The Descendants of
John Morgan and Mary Shaw

Compiled between 2011-2016

By

Lorin Morgan-Richards and Karen Marie Richards

Contributions by: Cecelia Watkins, Sean Sharp, Ron Morgan, Joe Morgan, and Tom Adkins

Morgan crest owned by Oscar W. Morgan Jr.

The motto of this crest is in Latin meaning "While I breathe, I hope."

Morgan Surname

The surname Morgan has several different British origins. The Welsh surname is derived from the Old Welsh personal name Morcant, which is of an uncertain origin. (A Dictionary of First Names. Oxford University Press. ISBN 0192800507).

The surname Morgan traces its origin from the powerful Welsh family established c.1330 by Morgan ap Llewelyn, (son of Llewelyn ap Ifor, Lord of St. Clere, and Angharad, daughter and heiress of Sir Morgan ap Maredudd (Meredith), Lord of Tredegar) and is of Welsh origin, meaning either "great kingdom" or "great hundred".

It is a popular family name in Wales, as well as there being a group of Morgans from "Morgund". According to the crest source, since early times they were chiefly in southern Wales in the shire Carmarthen. It is possible that the name was Celtic from the Cornovii Tribe who lived in the North of Scotland and in the Severn Valley near the Wrekin in Shropshire. The County of Glamorgan is named after the Princes of South Wales named Morgan, a group, part of which developed into the name Leyshon. The term for water sprites in Welsh is morgans (Tongue, Ruth L. (1970) Forgotten Folk-Tales of the English Counties Routledge & Kegan Paul, London, p. 27).

Emigration Patterns from Wales

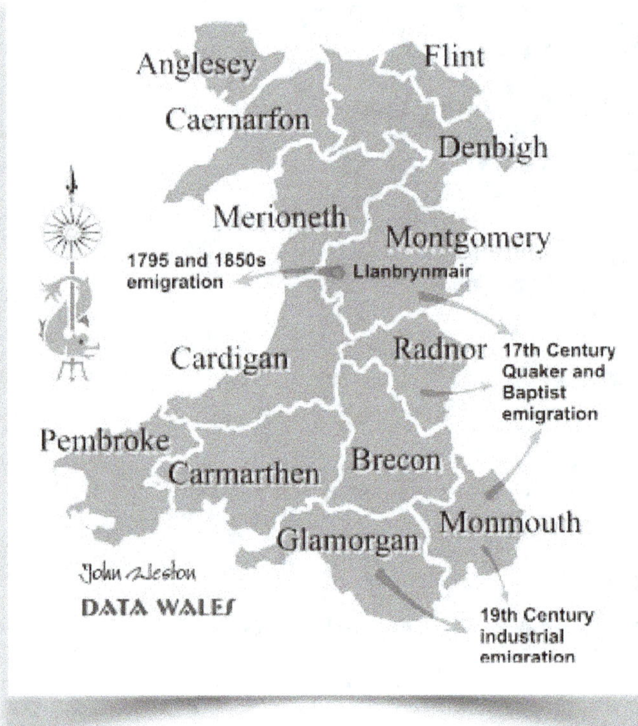

One of the first Welsh settlers was Howell Powell who left Brecon for Virginia in 1642. In 1660 Charles II was restored to the English throne and religious intolerance increased.

Llanbrynmair became a noted source of emigrants to America as a result of the enthusiasm of a local cleric.

The bulk of Welsh emigrants to America left via the English ports of Bristol and Liverpool.

The Departure Point of Liverpool

In the 19th Century, thousands of emigrants from the British Isles and mainland Europe left from Liverpool. The establishment of regular sailing packet lines from 1818 and the huge demand for North American timber and cotton as raw materials for British industry led to well established transatlantic links, and emigrants, along with British manufactured products provided a useful return cargo.

Emigrants were not allowed on board their ships until the day before, or the actual day of sailing, so this meant that most emigrants usually spent between one and ten days waiting for their ship in a Liverpool lodging house.

*Until the early 1860s most emigrants left Liverpool on a sailing ship. The voyage to the US and Canada took about thirty-five days. Most emigrants traveled in the cheapest accommodation, known as the steerage. This was similar to a dormitory with bunks down the sides and tables in the centre. It was frequently overcrowded with poor ventilation. Emigrating in a sailing ship could be unpleasant, particularly during a storm. Seasickness was a particular problem on the stormy North Atlantic westbound voyage. Diseases such as cholera and typhus frequently reached epidemic proportion as infection spread through the confined decks. Scores of emigrants died on this account. Conditions on emigrant ships were covered by a series of Passenger Acts which attempted to lay down minimum standards of accommodation, rations and sanitation (*liverpoolmuseums.org.uk*).*

John Morgan's journey from Wales to America

While we are lacking exact details as to how our ancestor John Morgan made the voyage from Wales, we do know that from his stout religious perspective he came as a Methodist or religious reformer and that his journey must have taken place sometime between 1801 and the early 1820's. Judging by census records, he is presumed to have spent his youth in Pennsylvania. Evidence of his birthplace is seen in the 1900 and 1910 Greenup, Kentucky census records where his son

Ephraim and family have documented, as well as the death certificate of Josiah S. Morgan. It is of note that Ephraim must have been very close to his mother, caring for her until death. Records state his father, John Morgan, was born in Wales and his mother, Mary Shaw, born in New Jersey.

During the time of John's birth, Calvinistic Methodists along with other religious groups were fleeing from the uncompromising doctrine of the Church of England. Along with the promise of land and idealistic opportunities Pennsylvania and the Ohio Valley were idyllic. The large emigration patterns from Wales also influenced William Penn's original idea of titling Pennsylvania "New Wales". Both Pennsylvania and the Ohio Valley however were not unoccupied and several Native American cultures clashed with the encroaching military and settlers who were destroying their life ways. The drive westward continued into an area called the Seven Ranges (Old Seven Ranges), which included the future Carroll and Columbiana counties. Public land sales of this region began in 1787 in Philadelphia, Pittsburgh, New York and Steubenville, Ohio. By 1795, the Treaty of Greenville compromised the Native Americans into losing their land and opened up settlement in Ohio at a heightened pace. Steubenville was founded shortly after in 1797, and the land office there opened in 1801. The Steubenville Land Office was responsible for sales in the northern part of the tract, within 48 miles (77 km) of the Geographer's Line. The Marietta Land Office sold lands in the southern part. Settlers of these tracts were primarily from Pennsylvania and Virginia.

Unfortunately, records up to 1830 are speculative to say the least. The first record for John Morgan begins with the marriage of Mary Shaw in 1826 in Columbiana County, Ohio. The United States federal census for Ohio goes to 1820, but not fully noted in 1810. The 1820 records shows Morgan's of Hamilton Co. and the Symmes seizure in Ohio (see section titled **Notes**). Other records, such as the US Census Reconstructed Records 1660-1820 for example, of the time do not contain enough information to track. We can see early settlers of Columbiana, Ohio and nearby regions before 1820 included:

- 1810 William Morgan of (no twp listed), Columbiana, Ohio
- 1820 Isaac Morgan of Wayne, Columbiana, Ohio
- 1820 Lewis Morgan of Wayne, Columbiana, Ohio
- 1820 Robert C Morgan of Wayne, Columbiana, Ohio
- 1820 Samuel Morgan of Fox, Columbiana, Ohio
- 1820 Thomas C Morgan of Fairfield, Columbiana, Ohio
- 1820 William Morgan of Wayne, Columbiana, Ohio
- 1810 Charles Morgan (He is the original proprietor(?) of land owned in 1810 by Nathe Beasley.) Ohio (no distinct area)
- 1810 Daniel Morgan (He is the original proprietor(?) of land owned in 1810 by Andrew Ellison) Ohio (no distinct area)
- 1810 John Morgan (He is the original proprietor(?) of land owned in 1810 by John Fisher)
- 1810 John Morgan (He is the original proprietor(?) of land owned in 1810 by Andrew
- Ellison) – of note, this may show a relation to Daniel of 1810. Ohio (no distinct area) 1810 Jonas Morgan (He is the original proprietor(?) of land owned in 1810 by Joseph
- Darlington and Wm Geo Wilson) Ohio (no distinct area)
- William tax list for Columbiana, Ohio
- William tax list for Columbiana, Ohio
- 1790 Benjamin Morgan for Washington, Ohio
- 1790 John Morgan for Ohio Territory –Davidson Co. Tenn
- 1800 Isaac Morgan Northwest Territory Ohio
- 1800 Evan Morgan Northwest Territory Ohio
- 1800 John Morgan Northwest Territory Ohio
- John Sen Morgan Northwest Territory Ohio
- David Morgan Washington, Ohio
- Charles Morgan Army Lands –VA Military Dist (OH)
- 1801 John Morgan Army Lands –VA Military Dist (OH)

<u>In the 1830 Federal Census of Augusta Twp., Columbiana Co., Ohio</u> (later Carroll Co.) our John Morgan family appears based on the age and number of children and parents, surrounding known relatives, the marriage record, other persons of interest, and finally by process of elimination.

In this the John Morgan family is the sixth record from the bottom: 2 males under 5 (Nathan, Jeremiah), 1 male btw 20 and 30 (John Sr.), 1 female under 5

SCHEDULE of the whole number of Persons within the Division allotted to

FREE WHITE PERSONS, (INCLUDING HEADS OF FAMILIES.)

Name of County, City, Ward, Town, Township, Parish, Precinct, Hundred, or District: Augusta Township

MALES

NAMES OF HEADS OF FAMILIES	under 5	5 to 10	10 to 15	15 to 20	20 to 30	30 to 40	40 to 50	50 to 60	60 to 70	70 to 80	80 to 90	90 to 100	100, &c.
John Hemantinger				1					1				
John Marshall	1			1					1				
Jacob Marshall	2	1		1	1			1					
Charles Bowen	1	1					1						
Widow Crawford			1	1									
James Watson	2					1							
John Watson	1					1							
Widow Watson													
Jacob Long	2				1								
Thomas Herrington	2				1								
Solomon Long	1				1								
Mosey Long					1								
George Gassman	3				1								
James Martin			2			1							
John Myers		1	1	3		1							
William Vanpelt	1				1								
John Long			1				1						
Charles Packham	3	2	1			1							
Ephraim Hundell					1								
John Herrington				1	3		1						
Widow Hale		2											
John Herrington	1	1	1			1							
John Morgan	2					1							
Robert Maxwell		1	2	1			1						
John Downs					1			1					
James Grimes	1	1	1			1							
Jacob Starling					1			1					
Hugh Wilkison		1	1	1									
Total	**23**	**11**	**11**	**9**	**14**	**6**	**4**	**3**	**3**				

FEMALES

NAMES OF HEADS OF FAMILIES	under 5	5 to 10	10 to 15	15 to 20	20 to 30	30 to 40	40 to 50	50 to 60	60 to 70	70 to 80	80 to 90
John Hemantinger		1	1	1		1					
John Marshall			1	1			1				
Jacob Marshall		1	1				1				
Charles Bowen	2					1			1		
Widow Crawford		1	2	1	1		1				
James Watson	1	2					1				
John Watson	1						1				
Widow Watson						2			1		
Jacob Long	1		1			1					
Thomas Herrington	1		1			1					
Solomon Long	1					1					
Mosey Long						1					
George Gassman							1				
James Martin				1	2						
John Myers	2	1	1				1				
William Vanpelt	2	1					1				
John Long	2	1	1	2			1				
Charles Packham				1						1	
Ephraim Hundell							1			1	
John Herrington										1	
Widow Hale	1	2	1	1			1				
John Herrington	1	1	0	0			1			0	
John Morgan	1	1					1				
Robert Maxwell			1				1				
John Downs						2			1		
James Grimes	1	2		1	1					1	
Jacob Starling			1	1							
Hugh Wilkison										1	
Total	**16**	**17**	**10**	**13**	**11**	**7**	**6**	**4**	**2**		

(Ruth Ann), 1 female btw 5 and 10 (Lucinda Long), and a female btw 20 and 30 (Mary).

John Morgan is missing in the 1840 Augusta Twp., but with a few clues we can decipher where his family went.

Some noteable neighbors found in both Census Records for 1830 and 1840 Augusta Twp., Columbiana Co., Ohio:

A. John Marshall abt 1800-1810 (Augusta, Columbiana, OH)

B. James Watson 1790-1800 (Augusta, Columbiana, OH)

C. Solomon Long 1800-1810 (Augusta, Columbiana, OH)

D. John Herrington (Augusta, Columbiana, OH)

Keeping this in mind, we know that a Jabez or Jabeth Coulson was acting Justice of the Peace marrying John Morgan and Mary Shaw in 1826 in Columbiana, Co., Ohio. Jabez so happened to be listed in the same 1830 Augusta Township, Columbiana, Ohio census with our John Morgan family and related Longs, Shaws, and the Herringtons who formed the Herrington Bethel church (see cemetery records).

Portrait from the History of Columbiana County, Ohio: with illustrations and biographical sketches of some of its prominent men and pioneers.

In the 1840 East Twp., Carroll County, Ohio census - Jabez/Jabeth/Jabis Coulson, is found that he either moved or the township changed around him – which it had done in 1832. In 1832, Augusta Township went from Columbiana to Carroll changing its boundaries, partly splintering off into new townships.

Lets understand this better by looking at some of those around him in the 1830 census of Augusta Twp and see in parantheses where they lived in 1840:

A. Jabis Coulson appeared on page 11 of Augusta Twp.

Also on the page are the following:

B. Jacob Hole (in 1840 he lived in West, Columbiana)

C. William Vallentine (in 1840 he lived Massillon, Stark, Ohio)

D. Nathan Hole (in 1840 he lived in Elkrun, Columbiana)

E. James Chambers (in 1840 he lived in East, Carroll)

F. James McBride (in 1840 he lived in Hanover, Columbiana)

After subsequent searches, there is a John Morgan family that closely matches in Franklin Twp., Columbiana, Ohio and it is of note, that our Morgan's moved to Scioto, Ohio in 1844. Thus, the possibility of Franklin Twp. should not be ruled out.

We know that in 1840, our John Morgan family consisted of 6 children under 20 years of age and 2 adults between 30 and 40 years of age.

A simple search of the 1840 census list for John Morgan's in and around Columbiana, Ohio and Scioto, Ohio are the following:

- John Morgan - Franklin Twp., Columbiana, Ohio (a possibility).
- John Morgan – Wayne, Columbiana, Ohio (this family we have ruled out, see **Notes**).
- John Morgan – Washington, Carroll County, Ohio (this has 7 children under 20, and 2 adults, but they are all girls except 1 boy, and age of adults is older).
- Another possibility ruled out by age and number in household is that they were living with Mary Shaws parents - the Nathan Shaw family in 1840 Washington, Carroll County, Ohio.
- The 1840 Franklin Twp, Columbiana, Ohio census of a John Morgan family seems to be a match, having 2 males under 5 (this would be John, Josiah), 2 males btw 5-10 (this would be Jeremiah, Ephraim), 1 male 10 to 15 (this would be Nathan), and a male (this would be John) 30 to 40, a female 5-10 (this would be Ruth Ann), and female 30-40 (this would be Mary). The census seems to be correct except that Ruth Ann should be 12 years of age. But anyone doing genealogy knows that relying on census materials for exact ages prior to 1900 understands there could have been an error, especially between 1 or 2 years.

Males

NAMES OF HEADS OF FAMILIES.	Under 5	5 & under 10	10 & under 15	15 & under 20	20 & under 30	30 & under 40	40 & under 50	50 & under 60	60 & under 70	70 & under 80	80 & under 90	90 & under 100	100 & upwards
John McGary			2				1						
Enos McMullen	1								1				
Wm Morgan			3		1								
Enos McMullen jr	1			1									
Thos Welch	1					1							
John Brannon					3								
John Morgan	2	2	1		1								
Wm Graham				2			1						
Ezekiel Bevington	1	1	1		1								
John Beasly	1	2	1			1							
Wm Beasly Sr			1										
Wm Beasly						1							
Jonathan Brown	1				1								
Saml Brown													
Charles Irwin		1	2			1							
Hugh King			1		1		1						
John Wallace					1								
Thos King			1	1			1						
Jonathan McHarng					1								
Daniel McHarng	1				1								
Philip Williams							1						
John Williams	2	2	2		1								
Peter Stifforger				1									
Jacob Fox		2		1	1								
Hugh Laughlin	1	1		1									
Gideon Davis						1							
Patrick McCondy	1	1				1							
Jacob Motorcan	2		1	2		1							
Elias Williams			1	1	3	1							
David Stone				1									
Adam Lustard		1	1	1									

Females

NAMES OF HEADS OF FAMILIES.	Under 5	5 & under 10	10 & under 15	15 & under 20	20 & under 30	30 & under 40	40 & under 50	50 & under 60	60 & under 70	70 & under 80	80 & under 90	90 & under 100
John McGary	2	1	1	1		1						
Enos McMullen						1	1					
Wm Morgan							1		1			
Enos McMullen jr	1			1	1							
Thos Welch			1	2			1					
John Brannon							1					1
John Morgan		1			1		1					
Wm Graham									1			
Ezekiel Bevington	2		1			1						
John Beasly	1		1			1						
Wm Beasly Sr	2					1						
Wm Beasly									1			
Jonathan Brown	1					1						
Saml Brown												1
Charles Irwin	1	1		2	1		1					
Hugh King					1			1				
John Wallace												
Thos King						1						
Jonathan McHarng					1							
Daniel McHarng	2	1				1						
Philip Williams							1					
John Williams	1		1			1						
Peter Stifforger												
Jacob Fox	2		1	1								
Hugh Laughlin	2										1	
Gideon Davis						1		1				
Patrick McCondy	2	1	2	3		1						
Jacob Motorcan	1	1	2			1						
Elias Williams		1	2						1			
David Stone	1					1				1		
Adam Lustard	1			1		1						

A second possible clue goes back to the previously mentioned Jabez Coulson listing in 1840. We see that in the 1840 East Twp., Carroll County, Ohio census - a Mrs. Ann Morgan is found with 2 boys between 5 and 10, 1 boy between 20 and 30, 1 girl under 5, 1 girl between 5 and 10, 1 girl between 30 and 40. She would have resided in a nearby jurisdiction as our John Morgan. Could this Ann (b.1814) be a relative of our John?

Another possible relation is a William Morgan on the same census page of the 1840 Franklin Twp., Columbiana, Ohio census that is of the same age. Although this William Morgan family was not on the 1830 Augusta Twp. census like our John Morgan family, his family did show up in the 1850 census of Franklin Twp., Columbiana Co., Ohio. According to the record his family was a- William Morgan b. 1800 in PA, a farmer, Catherine b. 1800 in PA, Jason b. 1827 in Ohio, a farmer, and Daniel b. 1828 in Ohio, a farmer.

Studying this William Morgan family further for answers- The 1860 census of Franklin Twp., Columbiana, Ohio has: Catherine (b.1804), James (b. 1827) Daniel (b.1829), Sidney (b.1822), Sarah (b.1848) and William D. (b. 1860), William Sr. is apparently deceased.

The same family in 1870 census of Franklin Twp., Columbiana, Ohio consisted of: Catherine (b.1817) -[this may be a huge error on the part of the census taker], Daniel (b.1828), William D. (b. 1862), Mary (b.1866) [not sure this is William's child, or adopted, or rather the following people's child living with Catherine: John Miller, (farm laborer), and Susan Boil (domestic servant).

Again in 1880 census of Franklin Twp., Columbiana, Ohio - Catherine Morgan family Catherine (b.1804), Daniel (b.1828), Annie (b.1839), and William D. (b. 1860), also listed are a Samuel Lindersmith and Mandy Jane Myers.

Staying with this family, in the 1900 census, there is a Daniel Morgan family – Daniel Morgan born March 1828 in Ohio to parents having been both born in PA. He married in 1873 to his wife Annie born in May of 1845.

So the question may be, is William Morgan a brother or cousin of our John Morgan? Having resided in the same township, both having lived in PA, near in age. Makes one wonder, but there is no definitive answer.

Researching we find the marriage of a William Morgan and a Catherine Lindersmith on March 23, 1826 as well as family tree records for their family on ancestry.com. Nothing however, shows who the parents were of William.

It seems that based on the names alone in the family that William, Jason and Daniel may not relate to our John Morgan but rather relate to the Wayne Twp. Morgan's (see Notes) but this is entirely uncertain. We do know that Franklin Twp added land from Wayne Twp in 1823.

Just to be certain, I looked back at the census of 1830 for Franklin Twp., but could not find a John Morgan. **Supporting the theory John Morgan moved or the township changed as it had in 1832**.

Therefore our John Morgan was listed in the 1830 census under Augusta Twp., and then by 1840 the twp of Franklin was created and they became incorporated into this. In 1832, parts of Columbiana became Carroll County. I

Name						
James Long	1	40	2	16	—	56
William Long	2	80	2	16	—	96
Solomon Long	2	80	2	16	—	96
Jacob Long	1	40	2	16	—	56
John Long	2	80	4	32	—	112
Jane McBride	—	—	4	32	—	32
James McBride	2	80	3	24	+	104
Stephen McBride	1	40	—	—		40
Wm Mercer	1	40	2	16	—	56
George Monahan	2	80	2	16	—	96
Enoz Monahan	1	40	1	08	—	48
James McClintin	2	80	4	32	—	112
Francis Moore	—	—	1	08	—	08
Samuel Miller	1	40	2	16	—	56
Roger Morledge	2	80	6	48	—	128
John Morledge	1	40	3	40	—	80
Robert Maxwell	3	120	2	16	—	136
John Morgan	1	40	2	16	—	56

Our John Morgan listed in the Ohio Tax Records, 1800-1850, for the year 1830 Augusta Township, Columbiana, Ohio

Name						
James Long	1	40	1	8	-	48
John Long	2	80	4	32	-	112
Solomon Long	2	80	1	8	-	88
William Long	2	80	4	32	-	112
Stephen Mansfield	1	40	2	16	-	56
Jeremiah McBride		80	3	24	-	104
Roger Morley	2	80	5	40	-	120
John Morlego	1	40	5	40	-	80
George Mansfield		40	7	56	-	96
John Mien			5	40	-	40
Jacob Marshall	1	40	5	40	-	80
John Morgan			3	24	-	24
Robert Marshall	2	80	2	16	-	96
James McBride	3	104	22	-	152	

Our John Morgan again listed in the Ohio Tax Records, 1800-1850, for the year 1831 Augusta Township, Columbiana, Ohio. Notice he is again neighboring Long families.

then looked at the 1820 census of Augusta Twp. Here, there are Crawford's and Long's, but no Morgan. This made me think his family had not settled in the area until after 1820. We do know that he married Mary Shaw in 1826.

Our John Morgan again listed in the Ohio Tax Records, 1800-1850, for the year 1832 Augusta Township, Columbiana, Ohio.

Our John Morgan is now listed in the Ohio Tax Records, 1800-1850, for the year 1834 Augusta Township, in what has changed to Carroll Co., Ohio

Name						
McBride Samuel	5	15	10	W. N.W.	69	79
Morlege John	5	15	19	S. E.	158	201
Morlege Roger	5	15	20	S. W.	120	166
do do	5	15	20	W. N.W	80	95
do do				Brewery		40
Miller Samuel	5	15	8	E pt N.W.	80	79
McBride Jeremiah	5	15	7	S. E.	117	151
McClintock James	5	15	4	S. W.	153	151
Morgan William	5	15	10	N. E.	160	189
Myers John	5	15	22	E S.E.	80	126
do do	5	15	22	W.S.E.	40	55
Manful William Sr	5	15	22	pt N.E.	121	190
Manfull William Jr	5	15	21	E S.E.	78	79
Mick Andrew	5	15	26	S pt N.W	76	97

By 1835, our John Morgan loses details in the tax records, replaced in the general area by a William Morgan. Ohio Tax Records, 1800-1850, for the year 1835 Augusta Township, Carroll Co., Ohio.

Between 1835 and 1838 John Morgan is no longer in the listing surrounded by his neighbors as it had been since at least 1830. Instead a William Morgan is now residing in Augusta Township, Carroll Co., Ohio in the same order John would have appeared. Could John have also gone by the name of William? Or could he have moved and issued or sold his land to a relative?

Most importantly, that from a 1846 Carroll County newspaper (Carroll Free Press) it shows a John Morgan was delinquent as of 1845 in paying taxes for 3 lots in Mechanicstown, Fox Twp, Carroll County. (At the time he moved to Scioto based on the birth of their son James Knos Morgan in Scioto) The newspaper is stating for those listed that their land is for sale as of 1846 for their delinquency. Leading to John either has to move because of this or that he already moved and that is the reason he is delinquent. See an excerpt from the newspaper on the following page:

Fox Township.

Name				Description	Acres	Value	$	cts	
Bakely Joseph	4	13	15	w. ½ s. e. qr.	80	109	4	82	Crissman, F
Boice John	4	13	22	n. part s. w. qr.	109	155	6	87	Cook, Samu
Johnson Nancy	4	13	33	part s. e. qr.	38½	48	2	13	Hawk, Robe
Morgan Samuel	4	13	11	s. e. qr.	160	242	10	72	Hardesty, V
McAllister Archer	4	13	20	part e. half s. w. qr	1	3		12	same
same				Tannery		145	6	42	Hentzell, Ja
McKee John	4	13	7	n e of n e qr	40	45	1	99	same
Stephenson Robert	4	13	25	s e of n w	40	58	2	57	same
Stephenson Joseph	4	13	6	e half n. e	80	92	4	08	Jennings, S
Watt David	4	13	20	e half s. w	75	145	6	42	Marshall, L
Wallace John	4	13	13	s w of s e qr	40	49	1	73	Potter, Hon
Watt David & James.				Pulling, Carding, &c. Factory,		358	15	85	Taylor, Pit
									Vail, Lewis

Town Lots.

Name				Description		Value	$	cts	
Boice John	No. 3			Mechanicstown		10		43	same
same		House		do		29	1	28	Vail, Davis
McAllister Archy	" 6			do		8		35	Weston, F
McClain John G.	" 36			do		4		17	
Morgan John	" 37			do		2		9	
same	" 42			do		6		26	Baxter, He
same	" 43			do		6		26	Betner, Mi
Thompson John M.	" 35			do		3		13	Burger, Ni
Watt David	" 49			do		8		35	same
Lindsay John F.	" 1			Watsville,		3		13	same
same	" 10			do		3		13	Burger & V
Watt David	" 5			do		4		17	Crusler, C
same	" 7			do		5		22	Crumbecke
same	" 8			do		5		22	same
same	" 20			do		4		17	Grund, Co
same	" 21			do		3		13	Huston, G
same	" 22			do		3		13	Hentzell, J

1846 Carroll County newspaper (Carroll Free Press) shows John Morgan delinquent on land taxes.

Some interesting notes in looking over the <u>1840 census record of Jefferson, Scioto County, Ohio:</u> it is clear that our Morgan family was still in the Carroll County/ Columbiana County area around 1840 but left soon after. Interestingly, William Marsh, whom Jeremiah labored under in the 1850 Jefferson Twp., Scioto Co., Ohio census, is listed. Samuel Farmer and other Farmer's also noted.

<u>In the 1850 Jefferson, Scioto County, Ohio census</u> - Ephraim Morgan appears to be working as a farmer on the property of William Jones (note that although the census lists his birthplace as Vermont, I believe this to be in error as it is marked Ditto as much of the page starting with Ohio, except one Jane Jones (wife of the William Jones).

Looking over the <u>1860 census record of Jefferson, Scioto County, Ohio,</u> there was an obvious population boom took place as in 1840 there were just 6 half census pages and in 1860 there were 32 full pages. Outside of our John Morgan family that is listed no other Morgan's appear.

<u>A Timeline based on the facts about our John Morgan:</u>

- Between 1801 and 1821 John and/or his family travels from Wales to Pennsylvania. They settled in the new state before the family likely saw the Seven Ranges public sale notice and left to purchase land in Ohio.

- Between 1819 and 1821 Mary Shaw gives birth to her first child, a daughter, Lucinda Long (it is unclear if this was out of wedlock or if there were two different Lucinda's born)

- On April 19, 1821 Mary Shaw weds her first husband George Long in Columbiana, Ohio

- Between 1821 to 1825 John moves to and lived in Augusta Twp, Columbiana, Ohio. In 1823 George Long and Mary (Shaw) Long give birth to another child, a son, George Long Jr.

- In 1823 (later in the year) George Long is killed by his brother Jacob in a hunting accident. Between 1823 and 1826 John Morgan courts Mary (Shaw) Long, it is unclear where the Long children reside. Presuming by the 1830 census, Lucinda is still in the care of Mary.

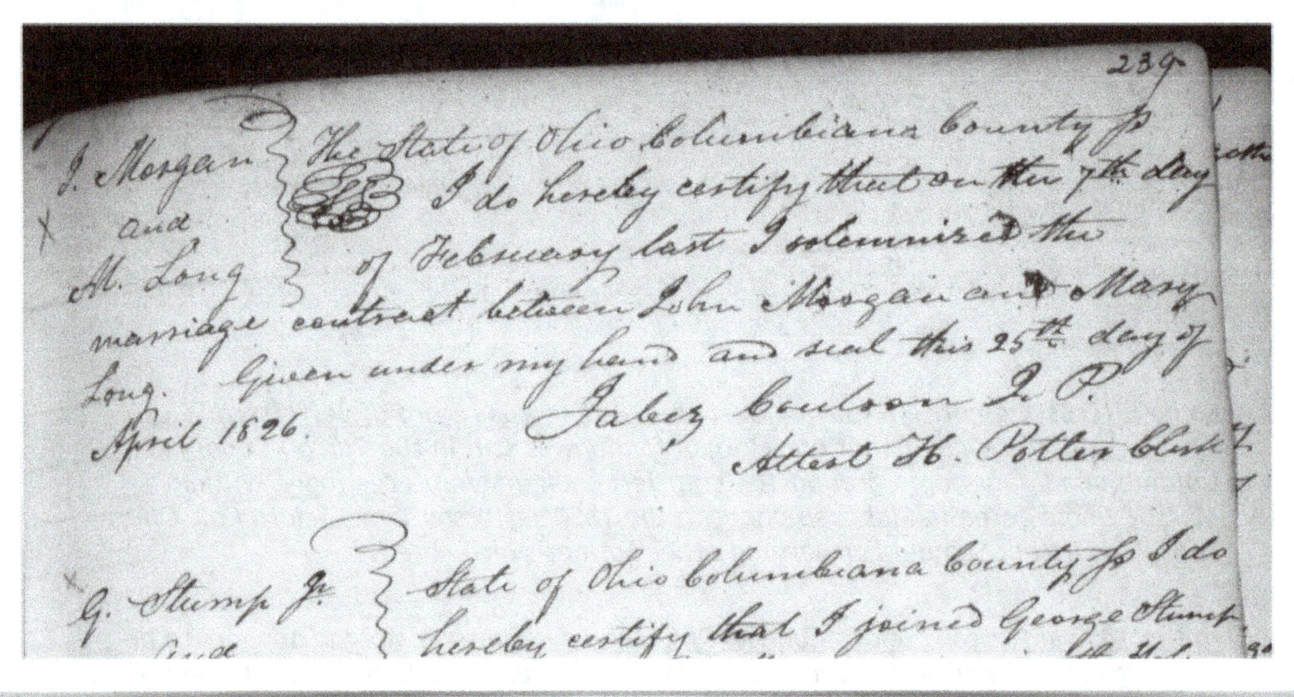

Marriage record of John Morgan and Mary (Shaw) Long: reads 'the state of Ohio Columbiana County. I do hereby certify that on the 7th day of February last I solemnized (performed) the marriage contract between John Morgan and Mary Long. Given under my hand and seal this 25th day of April 1826. Jabez Coulson J.P. (Justice of the Peace).'

- On February 7, 1826 John Morgan marries Mary (Shaw) Long in Columbiana, Ohio by Justice of the Peace Jabez Coulson.

- 1827 John Morgan and Mary have a son, Jeremiah.
- 1828 John and Mary have a daughter, Ruth Ann.
- 1830 John and Mary have a son, Nathan.
- 1830 the census is taken for Augusta Twp., Columbiana, Ohio listing numbers of John Morgan household.
- 1830 listed in Augusta Twp., Columbiana, Ohio
- 1831 listed in Augusta Twp., Columbiana, Ohio
- 1831 John and Mary have a son, Ephraim.
- 1832 listed in Augusta Twp., Columbiana, Ohio
- Between 1832 and 1834 Augusta Twp., Columbiana Co., Ohio ceded land to Franklin Twp., Columbiana, Ohio, part of Augusta Twp. becomes Carroll County.
- 1834 listed in Augusta Twp., Carroll Co.
- 1836 John and Mary have a son, John Jr.
- 1838 John and Mary have a son, Josiah Jr. in Columbiana Co.
- 1840 the census of Franklin Twp, Columbiana, Ohio lists numbers of John Morgan household
- 1841 John and Mary have a daughter, Sarah Catherine
- 1842 John and Mary have a son, Robert Dennison in Columbiana Co.
- 1844 John Morgan family moves to Jefferson Twp., Scioto County, Ohio.
- 1845 John Morgan is noted that he is delinquent on paying his land taxes in Mechanicstown, Fox, Carroll County, Ohio.
- In 1845, John and Mary have a son, James Knos in Scioto, Ohio.
- In 1850 census of Jefferson Twp., Scioto, Ohio. lists names of John Morgan and his family, <u>giving us a first real glimpse of details</u>.
- Between 1850 and 1860 Ephraim marries Eliza Farmer and moves to Greenup County, Kentucky. Nathan and Jeremiah move to Rio, Knox Co., Illinois and marry. Ruth Ann lives with her new husband Abner Field.
- In 1860 census of Jefferson Twp., Scioto, Ohio lists names of John Morgan and his family: John, Mary, John Jr., Josiah, Sarah, Robert, and James. (Josiah later moves to Greenup County to live with his brother Ephraim to farm).
- On Aug 15, 1862 John Morgan dies and is buried in the Morgan-Brown Cemetery, Jefferson Twp., Scioto, Ohio.
- Between 1862 and 1870 Mary Shaw moves to Greenup County, Kentucky to be in care of her son Ephraim. John Jr. moves to Greenup Co., Kentucky and marries Martha Gammon. James also moved to Greenup Co., Kentucky to live with his brother John Jr. to work on his farm. Robert Dennison, a student (possibly of ministry) in Jefferson Twp, is enlisted in the Civil War. Sarah Catherine married Henry Snyder.

- Around 1870, Mary Shaw writes and files her will in Greenup County, Kentucky.
- On Nov 26, 1870 Mary Shaw dies and the will is transferred to Scioto County, Ohio. She was buried beside her husband John Morgan in the Morgan-Brown Cemetery.
- Between 1870 and 1880 Nathan and Jeremiah made their way to Iowa.

John Morgan Sr.

Born: September 6, 1801 in Wales (raised in Pennsylvania)

Married: February 7, 1826, sealed on April 26, 1826 in Columbiana Co./Carroll Co., Ohio

Died: Aug 15, 1862.

Buried in Morgan-Brown Cemetery, Jefferson Twp., Scioto Co., Ohio (directly behind his home).

The 1860 Census of Scioto, Jefferson Twp., Ohio shows John as 59, which would verify the birth, date as 1801. His tombstone and Family Bible records now owned by Vida Besco granddaughter to Jeremiah Morgan also confirms this. John married Mary Shaw on February 7th and sealed by Jabez Coulson on April 25, 1826 in Columbiana Co., Ohio (see Columbiana Co., Ohio marriage records vol.2, pg.239). Also a census from Scioto County for 1850 lists the Morgan family with a Robert age 7 and tells how John worked as a millwright. Additionally, John was a founding trustee of the Blue Run Methodist Episcopal Church in Scioto, Ohio. The church was built in 1859, and Rev. Harrison Willis was the first pastor. Other trustees included James Varner and Milton Deselen. The original members of the church were John Morgan and wife; Abner Field and wife; Samuel Miller and wife; Jared Spriggs and wife; Eliza Varner, James Varner and wife and Mrs. Nancy Marshall. The Morgan family first settled on Rose Hill Road (approximately where the Pine Grove Church now stands) in the hilly area of Scioto, Ohio.

They donated the land for the Harger Cemetery and future Pine Grove Church. In September of 1859 they sold the land on Rose Hill Road to Thomas Dodds and moved to Blue Run Road. Across the road from where the Blue Run church now stands. They purchased the land from John and Olive Field. Part of this land was leased to Jefferson Township for the site of the Blue Run Methodist Episcopal Church. The amount paid being 10 cents a year for as long as it was used only as a place of worship.

Photo of church founded by John Morgan, opposite what was the old Morgan farm, Scioto, Ohio. Hill behind farm contains Morgan-Brown Cemetery where John and his wife Mary are buried.

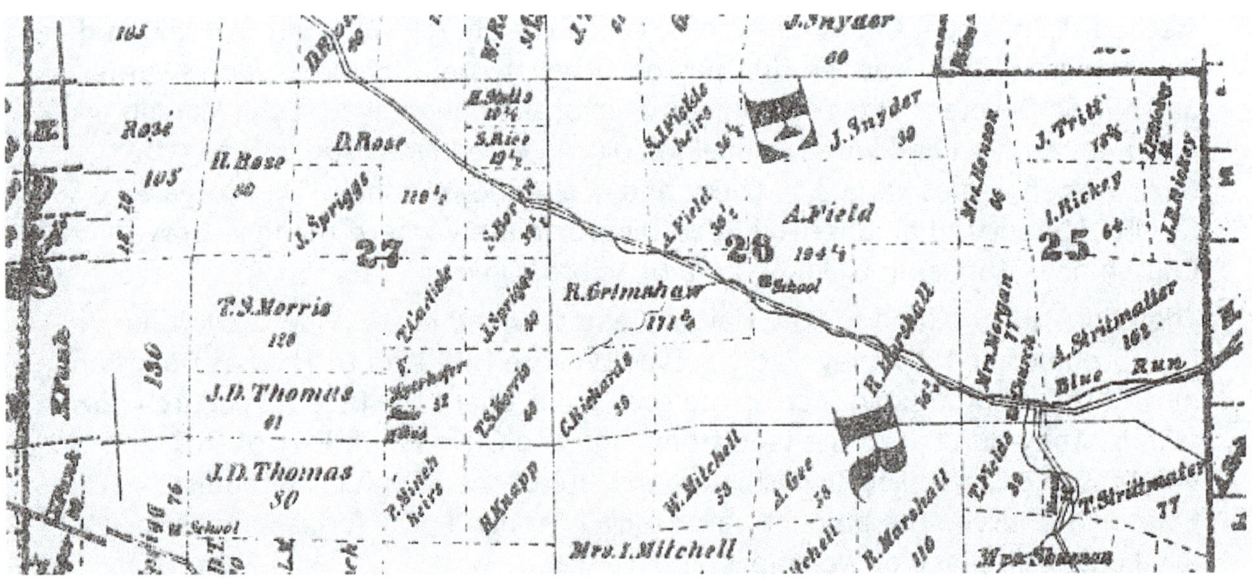

Map excerpt of Jefferson Twp., Scioto, Ohio in 1875 – on the right side you can see the former John Morgan farm property off Blue Run is in care of a Mrs. Morgan, the church is noted across the road (U.S. Geological Survey (7-1/2 Minute Quadrangle, Lucasville Sheet, 1961)

John's Wife: Mary Shaw

Born: Feb 15, 1803 in New Jersey (raised in Columbiana Co., Ohio)

Died: Nov 26, 1870. Buried in Morgan-Brown Cemetery, Jefferson Twp., Scioto Co., Ohio.

Father: Nathan Shaw

Mother: Ruth Crawford

Other Spouses: George M. Long

Mary Shaw's maternal line was Scottish. Her family was also Quakers and belonged to the Hopewell Society in Fayette Co., Pa. The church kept society records stating that in 1781 Josiah Crawford and his wife Cassandra joined the society along with eight of their ten children. All of the children are named except Sarah and Ruth they were not born yet.

Mary married her 1st husband George Long on April 19, 1821 in Columbiana Co., Ohio. George Long died two years later when he was accidentally shot by his brother Jacob hunting a wounded deer. Mary had 2 children by her first husband, George Long Jr. and Lucinda Long. In 1826, Mary married John Morgan, and the two had seven children in the Columbiana County area. Mary waited until her first two children (George Jr. and Lucinda Long) were grown and of age before relocating with John and family. Around 1844/5 they moved to Scioto Co., Ohio to live. After John's death, she went to live with her son Ephraim, who cared for her in Greenup Co., Kentucky. Her last will and testament was filed in Greenup County and then transferred to Scioto Co., Ohio. Many of the Shaw and Long family relatives are buried in the Herrington Bethel Cemetery in Augusta Twp., Carroll Co., Ohio. George Long was the first to be interred here. Also found here are the parents of Mary Shaw; Nathan Shaw and Ruth Crawford.

Simple gravestone marks George Long, first husband of Mary Shaw.

Other Shaw's listed in the Herrington Bethel Cemetery: *Dr. JM Shaw (d. 1873), Sarah (d. 1839), Alginus (d. 1841), Hannah (d. 1881), Nathan Corwin (d. 1884), Sarah (d. 1851), John H. (d. 1875), Henry Grove (b. 1850 d. 1935), Nathan L. (b. 1820 d. 1905), Lucinda (d. 1881), Harriet (d. 1848), Phoebe, Elisabeth (d. 1873), Juliann (d. 1845), Nathan (d. 1853), Elizabeth (d. 1880), Blanch Schooley (b. 1855 d. 1930), Ruth (d. 1836 - wife of Nathan), Richard (d. 1851), N.E. (d. 1842), Mary (d. 1899), Joshua (d. 1865), John G. (d. 1851), Sarah (b. 1823 d. 1909), Mary (b. 1850 d. 1924), Mary L. (d. 1883).*

Herrington Bethel Church and Cemetery. Church was built in 1843 after the original wood structure burned down. The current church is still active, a nice reminder of the area where Mary Shaw and her family congregated.

Karen Richards takes a photo of her son and fellow genealogist Lorin Morgan-Richards, beside the gravestones of Nathan Shaw and Ruth Crawford at the Herrington Bethel Cemetery.

1	2	3 — The Name of every Person whose usual place of abode on the first day of June, 1850, was in this family.	4 — Age.	5 — Sex.	6 — Color.	7 — Profession, Occupation, or Trade of each Male Person over 15 years of age.	8 — Value of Real Estate owned.	9 — Place of Birth.	10	11	12	13
		Timothy Miller	19	m		Farmer		Ohio				
		Mary D. Do	13	f				Do				
		Samuel G. Do	10	m				Do				
		Phebe A. Do	8	f				Do				
	1	John Morgan	49	m		Farmer	700	Pa				
		Mercy Do	48	f				Ohio				
		Jeremiah Do	24	m		Do		Do				
		Ruth M Do	22	f				Do				
		Nathan Do	21	m		Do		Do				
		Ephraim Do	19	m		Do		Do				
		John Do	13	m				Do		///		
		Josiah Do	11	m				Do		///		
		Sarah Do	9	f				Do				
		Robert Do	7	m				Do				
		James Do	5	m				Do				
	2	John Green	40	m		Farmer	700	Ireland				
		Lavina Do	38	f				Ohio				
		Sarah J. Do	17	f				Do				
		Susan Do	16	f				Do		///		
		James Do	17	m		Do		Do		///		
		Charlotte Do	15	f				Do		///		
		Mary J. Do	13	f				Do		///		
		John D. Do	11	m				Do		///		
		Eliza Do	9	f				Do		///		
	3	James Varner	60	m		Do	1000	Ireland				
		Elizabeth Do	72	f				Do				
	4	James S Do	36	m		Farmer		Ohio				
		Levisa Do	27	f				Do				
		Elizabeth Do	5	f				Do				
		Maria Do	3	f				Do				
		John Do	1	m				Do				
	5	Mark Snyder	47	m		Farmer	3000	Va				
		Betsey M Do	40	f				Do				

John Morgan and family listed in the 1850 Census of Jefferson Twp., Scioto Co., Ohio. 5th line from top. John is listed as a farmer.

a. First Child of John and Mary: Nathan Morgan

Born: Feb 26, 1830 in Columbiana Co., Ohio

Died: Apr 16, 1923 in Stuart, Iowa. Buried April 18, 1923 in Block 13, Lot 30, Space 3, Stuart Cemetery, Stuart, Guthrie Co., Iowa.

Married: Dec 29, 1853 in Henry Co., Ill. (or Knox

Co., Ill.)

Spouse: Lois Miranda (Slauson) Holmes:

b. Btw Dec 12 and 18th, 1838 near Westerlo, Albany Co., NY, d. May 26, 1917. Buried in Stuart Cemetery with husband.

Her father was a John Slauson/Slawson who was born in New York, and a mother Eliza A. Holmes also born in New York. Interestingly, later in life she must have taken on her mother's maiden name (reasons being unknown).

Nathan and Lois had the following children:

1. Ida M., b. Mar 28, 1857; d. before 1860 as an infant.
2. Oscar Winfield Sr., b. Jan 20, 1861 in Gailsburg, Illinois, d. Sep 29, 1934 in Stuart, Iowa. Cause of death being Bright's Disease.
3. Jesse S., b. Apr 2, 1859, d. before 1860, as an infant.
4. Delia Evaline, b. Feb 17, 1855 in Galesburg, Illinois, d. Dec 11, 1926 in Stuart, Iowa.
5. unknown, b. Jan 20, 1867, d. Jan 20, 1867.

Around 1852/3, Nathan and his brother Jeremiah traveled west. They stopped in Illinois where Nathan met and married his wife Lois. They settled for a short term; while Jeremiah went on to live in Taylor Co., Iowa. Nathan later moved with his family to Stuart County, Iowa. Nathan was a farmer.

Timeline:

In the 1860 Galesburg, Knox, Illinois census Nathan Morgan (age 26) is listed with his wife Lois (age 20), and Adelia (age 5). Nathan is a farm laborer.

July 1, 1863 Nathan Morgan (age 34) is listed as a farmer that is married and a resident of Rio in the 5th Congressional District of Illinois (Civil War Registration Record, 1863-1865 page 64).

(L to R) son Oscar Winfield Sr., Nathan, daughter Delia, and wife Lois

In a record for 1870 Rio, Knox, Illinois: Nathan Morgan (age 40), wife Lois (age 31), Delia (age 15), Oscar (age 9), Henry McLaughlin (age 17), Lewis Slawson (age 21), Charles Slawson (age 15), Jessie Slawson (age 22), Jessie Slawson (6 months). (Ancestry.com has these Slawson's incorrectly marked Lawson). Nathan is a farmer, Delia is at school, Charles Slawson is also at school. Henry McLaughlin is a farm hand.

137	137	Murray David	24	M	W	Farm hand			Va			1		1
		Irene	22	F	W	Keeping house			Ky				1	
138	138	Morgan Nathan	40	M	W	Farmer	6400	3800	Ohio					1
		Lois	31	F	W	Keeping house			N.Y.					
		Delia	15	F	W	at school			Ill			1		
		Oscar	9	M	W	"						1		

The 1870 Census of Rio, Knox, Illinois shows parents Nathan and Lois living with son Oscar (age 9), and daughter Delia (age 15). Nathan is a farmer, Lois is keeping house, and Delia is attending school.

1880 District 146, Rio, Knox, Illinois. Nathan Morgan (age 50), wife Lois (age 41), daughter Adelia Woodman (age 25), son in law J. Edward Woodman (age 28), granddaughter Lois (age 3 months), son Oscar (age 19). Nathan and J. Edward are farmers. Oscar is a farm hand. Nathan incorrectly has his father's

Morgan home in Stuart, Iowa

birthplace as PA and his mother PA.

In 1883 Nathan and family move to Iowa - according to the 1915 Iowa Census.

1895 Lincoln, Adair, Iowa. Nathan Morgan (age 65), Lois M. (age 56), and Oscar W. (age 34). (Iowa State Census Collection, 1836-1925). Nathan is marked a farmer, and Methodist.

division of county _______ [Insert name of township, town, precinct, district, or other civil division, as the case may be. See instructions.] _______ Name of Institution, _______ X

ated city, town, or village, within the above-named division, _____ Stuart city _____ Ward of city, _____

Enumerated by me on the _____ 1st _____ day of June, 1900, _____ Angson D. Moulton _____, Enumerator.

NAME	RELATION.	PERSONAL DESCRIPTION.								NATIVITY.			CITIZENSHIP.			OCCUPATION, TRADE, OR PROFESSION		EDUCATION.			
of each person whose place of abode on June 1, 1900, was in this family. Enter surname first, then the given name and middle initial, if any. Include every person living on June 1, 1900. Omit children born since June 1, 1900.	Relationship of each person to the head of the family.	Color or race.	Sex.	DATE OF BIRTH. Month.	Year.	Age at last birthday.	Whether single, married, widowed, or divorced.	Number of years married.	Mother of how many children.	Number of those children living.	Place of birth of this Person.	Place of birth of Father of this person.	Place of birth of Mother of this person.	Year of immigration to the United States.	Number of years in the United States.	Naturalization.	Occupation.	Months not employed.	Attended school (in months).	Can read.	Can write.	Can speak English.
3	4	5	6	7		8	9	10	11	12	13	14	15	16	17	18	19	20	21	22	23	24

1900 Stuart, Guthrie, Iowa. Nathan Morgan (age 70 -b. Feb 1830), Lois M. (age 60 -b. Dec 1839), and Oscar (age 38 -b. Jan 1862). Marriage year for Nathan and Lois is marked 1854. Nathan lists incorrectly father's birthplace as Pennsylvania and mother correctly as New Jersey. Both Nathan and son Oscar are listed as Landlords.

1905 Stuart, Guthrie, Iowa. Card number 56 Nathan Morgan, card number 57 Lois M., card 58 Oscar W. (Iowa State Census Collection, 1836-1925).

1910 Stuart, Guthrie, Iowa. Nathan Morgan (age 80), wife Lois (age 70), daughter Delia Woodman (age 58). Note- this was an extremely blurry document, but Nathan's family begins on page 25 line 72. The family neighboring Nathan on line 75 is Oscar Morgan, wife Lily Mabel, son Nathan W. and daughter Lois.

1915 Stuart, Guthrie, Iowa. Nathan Morgan (age 85) is marked retired, married, Methodist, fathers birthplace PA, mothers New Jersey, and having been in Iowa for 32 years (Iowa State Census Collection, 1836-1925 page 1032).

Nathan and Lois relax in their Stuart home circa 1916/17 (est. based on the US World War I poster)

April 16, 1923 Nathan Morgan listed on page 162, birth date as Feb 26, 1830. Buried in South Oak Grove Cemetery in the town Guthrie. Comment on Tombstone is Husband of Lois M. (Iowa Cemetery Records / Tombstone Records of Guthrie County, Iowa).

Lois died May 26, 1917 of Pleural Pneumonia. Nathan and Lois are buried in Block 13, Lot 30, Space 1, of the South Oak Grove Cemetery, Stuart, Iowa

b. Second Child of John and Mary: Ephraim Charles (L.) Morgan

Born: Dec 10, 1831 in Columbiana Co., Ohio

Died: Jan 5, 1913 in Village of Limeville, Greenup County, Edgington, Kentucky

Married: Dec 20, 1855 in Scioto Co., Ohio

1st Spouse: Elizabeth "Eliza" Farmer

Married: Apr 9, 1878 in Greenup Co., Kentucky

2nd Spouse: Susan (Hawkins) Middaugh

Ephraim and Elizabeth Farmer had the following children:

1. Katherine Belle, b. May 7, 1861 in Springville, Greenup Co., Kentucky; d. Dec 31, 1921 in Portsmouth, Scioto County, Ohio. Buried on Jan 3, 1922 in Bennett Cemetery, Madison Twp., Scioto Co., Ohio.

2. James Ephraim, b. Mar 1868, Springsville, Greenup Co., Kentucky, d. Nov 9, 1935 in Portsmouth, Scioto Co., Ohio. Buried on November 11, 1935 in Old Mackoy Church Cemetery, Siloam, Kentucky.

3. John Samuel, b. December 23, 1855 in Jefferson Twp., Scioto Co., Ohio, d. July 15, 1931 in Limeville, Greenup Co., Kentucky. Buried in Siloam Cemetery.

   m.(1) Alice C. ? on 1883; b. Jun 1861, Kentucky; d. Oct 18, 1916, Lawrence Co., OH; m.(2) Rose Lee "Swearingin" Lambert on Jun 16, 1920, Greenup Co., Kentucky; b. Jul 12, 1868, Carter Co., KY; d. Jun 24, 1934, Limeville, Greenup Co., KY. Buried on June 26, 1934 in Globe Cemetery.

4. Mary Ellen, b. May 20, 1859 in Springsville, Greenup Co., Kentucky, d. Nov 23, 1924 in Springsville, Greenup Co., KY. Buried on Nov 25, 1924 in Siloam Cemetery.

5. Sallie A., b. Sept 1, 1870 in Springsville, Greenup Co., KY, d. Aug 28, 1898.

6. William H., b. May 10, 1862 in Springsville, Greenup Co., KY, d. Dec 23, 1901.

7. Absalom M. "Abner", b. Apr 25, 1866 in Springsville, Greenup Co., KY, d. Jan 7, 1946 in Green Co. Infirmary, Greenup Co., KY.

8. Josiah Joseph Jr. (after mothers death, and father remarried, he was adopted by his Uncle Josiah and Aunt Melissa Morgan), b. Dec 25, 1872 in Springsville, Greenup Co., KY, d. Aug 29, 1960 in Columbus, Ohio. Buried on Sept 1, 1960 in Lucasville Cemetery.

9. Catherine Belle (also adopted by Uncle Josiah and Aunt Melissa Morgan), b. 1863, d. 1921.

Ephraim and Susan Middaugh had the following children:

10. Lytle Thomas, b. Aug 10, 1878 in Springsville, Greenup Co., KY, d. Aug 24,

    1932 in Limeville, Greenup Co., KY. Buried in Mackoy-Old Christian Church Cemetery, cause of death being a self-inflicted gunshot wound to the head. m.

    Ethel D. Bush on Feb 10, 1904 in Greenup Co., KY, b. 1883 in Greenup Co., KY, d. Dec 19, 1977 in Ashland, Boyd Co., KY. Buried in Mackoy-Old Christian Church Cemetery.

11. Oliver D., b. Aug 17, 1882 in Springsville, Greenup Co., KY, d. May 10, 1944 in Butler Co., Ohio. Buried in Greenlawn Cemetery, KY.

Timeline:

of *Kentucky* enumerated by me, on the *18th* day of *August* 1860. *Marshal Beue* Ass't Marshal

Post Office *Springville*.

1	2	3	4	5	6	7	8	9	10	11	12	13	14
		Isaac Nelson	12	m		Domestic			Kentucky		1		
800	824	Ambrose Hunt	34	m		day labor		50	Kentucky				
		Amantha	26	f					Kentucky				
801	825	Robert Jordan	20	m		day labor		10	Kentucky				
		Jane	17	f					Kentucky				
802	826	Henbery Lee	37	m		farm labor		500	Virginia				
		Lucinda	36	f					Kentucky				
		William G	12	m									
		Martha E	8	f							1		
		Rosa E H	5	f							1		
		Ellen C	2	f									
		Edgar M Lee	6	m					Kentucky		1		
		Henry Chadwick	22	m		day labor			Newyork				
803	827	Ephraim Morgan	29	m		farmer		1005	Ohio				
		Eliza	26	f					Ohio				
		John S	3	m					Ohio				
		Mary E	1	f					Kentucky				
		Catharine Harmer	22	f		Domestic			Ohio				
		Dalia Harmer	13	f		Domestic			Ohio		1		
		Josiah Morgan	22	m		farm labor		200	Ohio				
		Henry Doty	11	m		Domestic			Kentucky		1		

1860 Census Record for Greenup, Kentucky: Ephraim Morgan and family

FORM 1.—CONSOLIDATED LIST of all persons of CLASS 1, subject to do military duty in the _Ninth_ Congressional District, consisting of the Counties of Ma[son]... and ... State of _Kentucky_ enumerated during the month of _September_ 1863, under _William C. Grier_, Provost Marshal.

RESIDENCE.		NAME.	AGE 1st July, 1863	WHITE OR COLORED.	PROFESSION, OCCUPATION, OR TRADE.	MARRIED OR UNMARRIED	PLACE OF BIRTH (Naming the State, Territory, or Country.)	FORMER MILITARY SERVICE.	REMARKS.
[District] No. 7	1	McKoy John S.	32	White	Farmer	married	Kentucky		
	2	McKoy H. Clay	30	"			"		
	3	McQuillon James	24	"		unmarried	"		
	4	Steddaugh James Jr	32	"	Laborer		"		
	5	Moler John	33	"	Farmer	married	"		
	6	Mathews Carlisle	22	"	Laborer		"		
	7	Middaugh Henry	27	"			Ohio		
	8	Mitchell John	21	"		unmarried	Kentucky		
	9	McQuillon Warner	21	"			"		
	10	McQuillon William	26	"			"		
	11	Morton A. Clay	34	"	Farmer	married	"		
	12	Mosley John	21	"	Laborer	unmarried	"		
	13	Hanson George	32	"		married	Virginia		
	14	Montgomery Alexander	21	"		unmarried	"		
	15	Morgan John	25	"			Ohio		
	16	Morgan Ephraim	32	"	Farmer	married	"		
	17	Morgan Josiah	23	"			"		
	18	Meres Larkin	26	"			Kentucky		
	19	McCoy Joseph	35	"			Ohio		
	20	McQuillon Samuel	35	"			Kentucky		

JAMES B. FRY,
Provost Marshal General U. S.,
Washington, D. C.

STATION: Headquarters 9th Cong. Dist. of _Kentucky_

DATE: _October 30th 1863_

William C. Grier

September 1863 Sub District, Kentucky, Class 1, Congressional 9th US Civil War Draft Registration Record (for Greenup, Mason, and Lewis, Kentucky)

Dec 20, 1855 Marriage of Ephraim Morgan and Eliza Farmer. D-23 (Marriage Records of Scioto County, Ohio, 1803-1860).

July 1, 1863 Ephraim is listed in the 9th Congressional District of Kentucky. Ephraim (age 32), a farmer, is listed with his brothers Josiah (age 23) and John (age 25) (Civil War Registration Record, 1863-1865).

1870 Precinct 2, Greenup, Kentucky. Ephraim Morgan (age 38), wife Eliza (age 36), John S. (age 12), Mary E. (age 11), William H. (age 9), Catherine (age 7), Absalom (age 4), James (age 2), and a James Taylor (age 18) who is a farm laborer. Ephraim is a farmer and John S., Mary and William are attending school.

Nov 14, 1874 wife Elizabeth Farmer is deceased.

April 9, 1878 Ephraim remarries to Susan (Hawkins) Middaugh in Greenup, Kentucky.

1880 District 42, Hunnewell, Greenup, Kentucky. Ephraim (age 46), Susan (age 36), William (age 18), step daughter Eddie Hawkins (age 10), son Lyttle (age 18 months). Ephraim is a farmer. His father's birthplace is marked Wales and mother New Jersey. Ephraim's son William works on the farm. Andrew Workman (age 19) is a boarder working on the farm.

In 1880, Ephraim was in his second marriage to Susan Middaugh. His first wife, Eliza died Nov 14, 1874 of consumption or lung fever. She is buried in Mackoy Old Christian Church Cemetery in Siloam, Greenup County, Kentucky.

1880 Census for Hunnewell, Greenup, Kentucky of Ephraim Morgan and family (father noted from Wales, mother from NJ)

1890 Sadly, for most families, there does not exist an 1890 census. These materials were destroyed in a 1921 fire of the Commerce Building basement. This lead to a protest for a more permanent National Archives.

TWELFTH CENSUS OF THE UNITED STATES.

SCHEDULE No. 1.—POPULATION.

Enumerated by me on the 13 day of June, 1900. Josiah B. Merrill, Enumerator.

1900 Springville District 47, Greenup, Kentucky of Ephraim Morgan and family

1900 Magisterial District 47, Springville, Greenup Co., Kentucky. Ephraim (age 68 –b.Dec 1831), Susan (age 56 –b. Feb 1844), Lytle (age 21 –b. Aug 1878), Oliver (age 17 –b. Aug 1882). Ephraim's father birthplace is marked Wales and mother New Jersey. Ephraim and his sons are farm laborers.

1910 Magisterial District 3, Greenup Co., Kentucky. Ephraim (age 78), and wife Susan (age 68). Ephraim's father birthplace is marked Wales, his mother New Jersey. There is something not discernable on the birthplace for his after the word - Wales. It appears to be shorthand. The "y" in Kentucky above it hangs down over this word and the "k" in New York below it interferes slightly. Based on other records on pages before and after marking it with Ireland, it seems to be "Eng O" for England Occupied. Thereby being fully Wales England Occupied. This would make sense as Wales, Ireland, and Scotland might include England at that time.

DEPARTMENT OF COMMERCE AND LABOR—BUREAU OF THE CENSUS

THIRTEENTH CENSUS OF THE UNITED STATES: 1910—POPULATION

1910 - Magisterial District 3, Greenup, Kentucky

Further information can be confirmed in the 1910 census, including how many times married, M2 (married twice) is listed for Ephraim Morgan.

Jan 5, 1913 Ephraim C. Morgan is reported deceased in Limeville, Greenup Co., Kentucky (Kentucky Death Records, 1852-1953, page 8). Death due to Brights Disease. Listed as a farmer. Father birthplace Pennsylvania, Mother birthplace Ohio (both of which are incorrect). Ephraim was buried in Mackoy Old Christian Church Cemetery.

Jan 5, 1913 Death Record for Ephraim Morgan in Greenup, Kentucky. Notice the contradicting/incorrect birthplace of mother and father.

c. Third Child of John and Mary: Jeremiah Morgan

Born: Jan 30, 1827 in Columbiana Co., Ohio

Died: Aug 29, 1909. Buried in Plattsville, Iowa Cemetery, Taylor co., Iowa

Spouse: Elizabeth Neu

Married: Dec 30, 1859 (to Mary)

Spouse: Mary Magdalene Prospt

Jeremiah and Mary Prospt had the following children:

1. Mary Susan, b. Jan 1861, d. Jan 1866, death caused by Diptheria.

2. Adam Alvin, b. Dec 1863.

3. Hannah Catherine, b. Jan 1866, born same day sister died.

Jeremiah moved to Scioto Co., Ohio around the age of 17 and helped his father on the farm to raise his family. About 1858, he took his savings and put it in a belt around his waist and along with his brother Nathan went west.

Stopping shortly in Illinois, he then moved on to Taylor Co., Iowa. Where he purchased land and settled. He met and married his wife Mary Magdalene Prospt and had three children. As of 2010, Viola Besco, granddaughter to Jeremiah Morgan, now holds the family Bible records.

(Sources: Family Bible, Marriage- Taylor Co., Iowa Marriage Book #1 page 52. Death Notice from Taylor Co., Iowa Vol. 3 page 30. Census 1850 Scioto Co., Oh and 1860-1880 Taylor co., Iowa Gravesite in Plattsville Cem. Taylor Co., Iowa. Newspaper clippings from Plattsville paper 1858 with Family History Written by his Granddaughter Hazel Morgan Blaine. Land record for Mary Morgan's land Vol. 24 page 142 he is also named in his mother's will.)

Timeline:

1850 Jefferson, Scioto, Ohio. Jeremiah Morgan (age 24) is listed under John Morgan and family on census date of August 14, 1850 collected a Mr. Chandler.

Also in 1850 Jefferson, Scioto, Ohio. Jeremiah Morgan (age 23) is listed under the William Marsh family as a laborer on census date of August 15, 1850 collected by a Mr. Chandler.

Note - My assumption is Jeremiah reported to work at the Marsh farmstead on this day, and the age discrepancy is that the head of the household reported the names and their ages to the census taker.

Between 1850 and 1860 Jeremiah Morgan moves with his brother Nathan to Knox, Illinois then on to Taylor Co., Iowa. Nathan stays for several years in Knox, Illinois.

1860 Jefferson, Taylor, Iowa. Jeremiah (age 30) is listed under the household of James Sickles. Jeremiah is a carpenter.

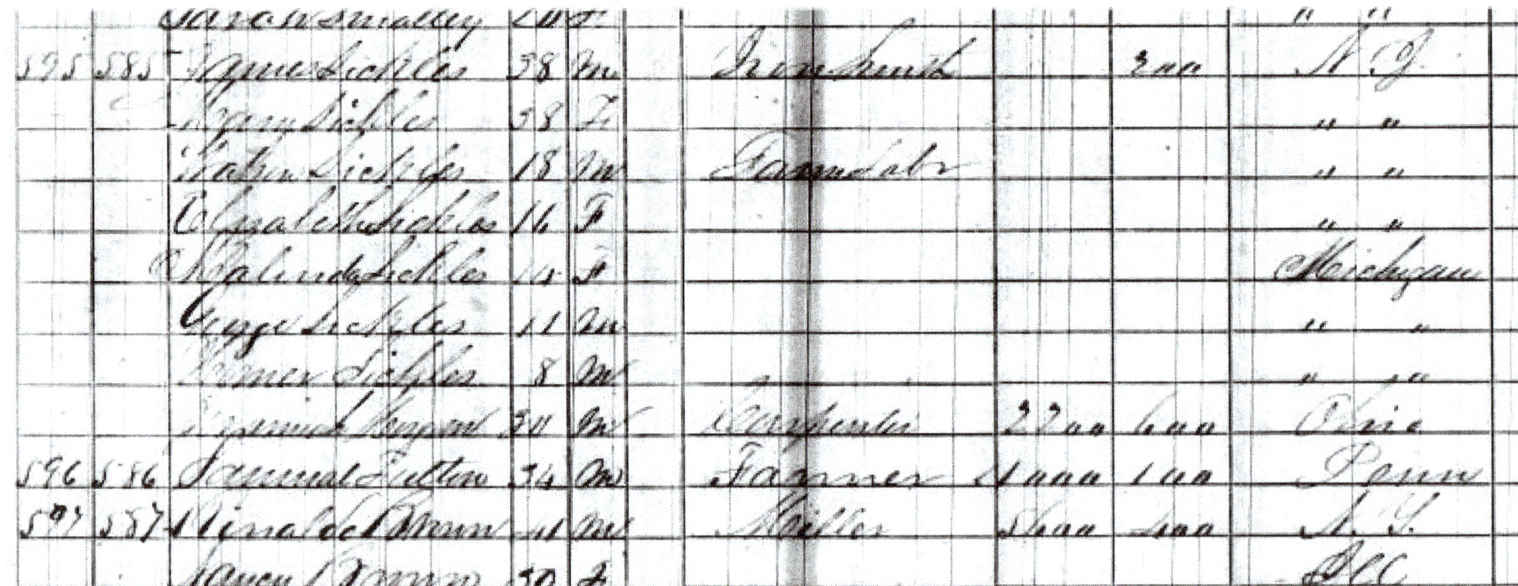

1860 Jefferson, Taylor, Iowa. Jeremiah listed under the household of James Sickles.

RESIDENCE	NAME	Age 1st July 1863	White or Colored	PROFESSION, OCCUPATION, OR TRADE	PLACE OF BIRTH (Naming the State, Territory, or Country.)	FORMER MILITARY SERVICE	
Doyle tp Clark Co	1 McCord William	36	White	Driver	Ohio		Resid
" "	2 McKee Francis M	38	"	Black Smith	Indiana		
Ward "	3 Meyer John P	37	"	Farmer	Ohio		
" " "	4 McCaw James H	39	"	"	Virginia		
Washington martin "	5 McGuire Spencer J	42	"	"	Indiana		
Marion "	6 Moosman Joseph H	38	"	"	Ohio		
Benton tp Taylor Co	7 McKendree Cain N	38	"	Minister	Pennsylvania		
Dallas "	8 McBride William	42	"	Farmer	"		
" " "	9 McLain John	43	"	"	Kentucky		
" " "	10 McAlpin Daniel	40	"	"	Tennessee	2 months 11th missouri boo	
Jefferson "	11 Murdock Hiral	40	"	"	Indiana		
" " "	12 Morgan Jeremiah	35	"	"	Ohio		

Line 12 – Jeremiah Morgan in 1863 Civil War Draft 5th Congressional District of Iowa

In 1863, Jeremiah (age 35) was listed in the Jefferson, Taylor, Iowa US Civil War Draft 5th Congressional District of Iowa.

1870 Jefferson, Taylor, Iowa. Jeremiah (age 40) is listed as a farmer, with wife Magdalene (age 30 born in Virginia), son Alvin A. (age 6), and daughter Hannah (age 4).

1885 Jefferson, Taylor, Iowa. Jeremiah (age 57) is a farmer, wife Mary M. (age 47), Alvin A. (age 21), Katie (age 18) (Iowa State Census Collection for 1836-1925).

1900 Jefferson, Taylor, Iowa. Jeremiah (age 74 -.b Jan 1827) marked widowed. Jeremiah is living with his son in law's family Geo L. Brown (age 30), H.C. (age 34), and May M. (age 7). H.C. in this case is Jeremiah's daughter Hannah.

On the same census page, we can see A. A. Morgan (Alvin age 35 –b. Dec 1864) is in a neighboring household with his wife S.E. (age 22-b.May 1878) and daughter Hazel (age 2 –b. May 1898)

1900 Census of Jefferson, Taylor, Iowa. Interestingly, Jeremiah's parents birthplace are marked unknown.

There is a detail that he married twice, with an Elizabeth Neu. However I was unable to find any record of this.

August 29, 1909 Taylor Co., Iowa. Date of death according to the Poore Family Tree, among others on ancestry.com.

d. Fourth Child of John and Mary: Ruth Ann Morgan

Born: Jun 9, 1828 in Columbiana Co., Ohio

Died: Dec 30, 1897. Buried in Morgan-Brown Cemetery, Colegrove Hill, Scioto Co., Ohio

Married: Feb 27, 1852 at her parents' home or the Blue Run Methodist Church in Scioto Co., Ohio
Spouse: Abner Field

Ruth Ann and Abner Field had the following children:

1. Mary Ellen Field, b. Jan 23, 1853, Scioto Co., OH, d. Sep 26, 1937, buried in Lucasville Cemetery, Lucasville, Scioto Co., Ohio. Mary Ellen never married, but lived with her mother and father until their deaths. She then lived with her sister Sarah until her death.

2. Sarah Ann Field, b. Apr 27, 1854, Scioto Co., OH, d. Feb 19, 1930, buried in Lucasville Cemetery, Lucasville, Scioto Co., Ohio.

3. Jeremiah M. Field, b. 28 Feb 1856, Scioto Co., OH; d. 27 May 1930, Bur. in Lucasville Cem. Lucasville, Scioto Co., Ohio; m. Joanna Funk.

4. Eliza Jane Field, b. 20 Nov 1857, Scioto Co., OH; d. 25 Jan 1890, Bur. Morgan-Brown Family Cemetery, Blue Run Rd. Scioto Co., Ohio, m. Robert Tumbleson/Tomlinson, 1876, Scioto, OH.

5. Melissa Catherine Field, b. 20 Jun 1860, Or 1861 in Scioto Co., OH; d. 03 Dec 1933, Bur. in Glendale Cemetery, Scioto Co., Ohio; m. John Shuman, Feb 17, 1881, Scioto, OH.

6. John Henry Field, b. 11 Oct 1863, Scioto Co., OH; d. 27 Mar 1897, Bur. Morgan-Brown Family Cemetery, Blue Run Rd. Scioto Co., Ohio, m. (1) unknown Brumfields, m. (2) Elizabeth "Olara" McCoy, Jul 2, 1892, Scioto,

    OH.

7. Rhoda Francis G. Field, b. Oct 29, 1865 (Or 10/29/1859) in Scioto Co., OH, d. Nov 29, 1937, buried in Martin Cemetery, Scioto Co., Ohio, m.

(1) John Robinette, m. (2) Henry B. Sherbourne, Mar 20, 1884, Scioto, OH.

8.   Nancy Ann Marie Field, b. Dec 4, 1867, Jefferson Twp., Scioto Co., OH, d. Mar 23, 1931, Jefferson Twp., buried in Lucasville Cemetery, Lucasville, Scioto Co., Ohio.

Ruth Ann was named after her grandmother Ruth Shaw as she was the first girl. Ruth Ann met her husband Abner Field in Scioto Co. Ruth Ann remained close to her parents and lived on Blue Run called "Nairan" at the time. She also attended the Blue Run Church. Her husband Abner was an elder and sang to close each church service.

Timeline:

Feb 27, 1852 Marriage of Ruth Ann Morgan and Abner Field. MA, B-231 (Marriage Records of Scioto County, Ohio, 1803-1860, Chapter F, page 43).

1860 Jefferson, Scioto, Ohio. Listed as Ann Field (age 32), Abner Field (age 30), Mary (age 7), Sarah (age 6), Jeremiah (age 4), Eliza (age 2). Abner is a farmer.

1870 Jefferson, Scioto, Ohio. Ruth A. Field (age 43), Abner (age 40), Mary E. (age 17), Sarah A. (age 16), Jermiah (age 14), and Eliza J. (age 12), Melissa (age 9), John H. (age 6), Rhoda (age 4), and Nancy (age 2). Abner is a farmer, and Jeremiah farm laborer.

1880 Jefferson, Scioto, Ohio. Listed as Ruth A. (age 52), Abner (age 50), Mary E. (age 27), Melissa (age 18), John (age 16), Roda (age 14), Nancy (age 12). Abner and John work on farm.

Dec 30, 1897 Ruth Ann is deceased.

e. Fifth Child of John and Mary: John Morgan Jr.

Born: Oct 10, 1836 in Columbiana Co., Ohio

Died: Jun 12, 1909 in Kings County, California.

Married: Oct 27, 1864 in Siloam, Greenup Co., KY
Spouse: Martha Elizabeth Gammon

John Jr. and Martha Gammon had the following children:

1. Harriet Frances, b. June 1, 1869, Greenup Co., KY, d. Nov. 16, 1940.
2. Annie, b. 1872 in Greenup Co., KY.
3. George W., b. Jan 1878.
4. Robert E., b. June 5, 1879 in Arkansas, d. Sept. 13, 1959 in Kings Co., California.

Sometime between 1860 and 1863, John Jr. relocated to Kentucky to live with his brother Ephraim. Here he worked as a farmer and met and married his wife Martha. In 1870, his brother James Knos is working and living with he and his wife. Harriet, daughter of John and Martha, is also listed at 2 years old.

According to the Morgan-Parrent Family Tree, John Jr.'s middle name started with R. (This is unconfirmed). His wife's full name was Martha Elizabeth Gammon. Martha was born Nov. 23, 1841 in Greenup Co., Kentucky. She died on Oct. 7, 1920 in Kings County, CA.

Timeline:

1863 John Jr. (age 25) was listed with his brothers Ephraim and Josiah in the US Civil War Draft 9th Congressional District of Kentucky (see previous image under Ephraim)

1870 Precinct No. 2, Greenup, Kentucky. Lists John Morgan Jr. (age 32) is a farmer, wife Elizabeth (age 28), Harriet (age 2), and brother James Knos (age 24) as a farm laborer. Harriet has an unusual birth location as Missouri. An Augustus Lamlin from Louisiana is also a farm laborer (age 26).

1880 Portsmouth, Dist. 171, Scioto, Ohio. John Morgan (age 42) is a carpenter, wife Martha (age 37), with children Hattie (age 12), Annie (age 8), George (age 5), Robert (age 3). John Jr. fails to give a location of birth for his father. His mother is listed as Ohio.

Between 1880 and 1900 John Jr. moved to California with his family. He was the first of the John Morgan descendants to move to California.

1900 Lucerne, Kings, California. John Jr. (63), wife Martha (age 53 –b. Nov 1846), children George (age 22 –b. Jan 1878) and Robert (age 20 –b.June 1879). John and Martha married in 1865. John is a house carpenter and sons are farm laborers.

June 19, 1909 in Lucerne, Kings, California. Date of death according to Morgan/Parrent Family Tree.

f. Sixth Child of John and Mary: Josiah S. Morgan

Born: Sep 27, 1838 in Columbiana Co., Ohio

Died: 25 Mar 1920. Buried in Lucasville Cemetery, Lucasville, Scioto Co., Ohio

Married: Abt. 1850

Spouse: Melissa Catherine "Kit" Farmer

Josiah and Melissa adopted Catherine and Josiah Joseph Morgan, Jr. (their niece and nephew) after their biological mother (Elizabeth) died and biological father (Ephraim) remarried. Josiah was named after his great grandfather Crawford and his uncle Josiah Shaw. Josiah and Ephraim Morgan married the daughters of Samuel and Catherine (Carlisle) Farmer. They lived in the Blue Run community also.

Timeline:

1863 Josiah (age 23) was listed with his brothers Ephraim and John Jr. in the US Civil War Draft 9th Congressional District of Kentucky (see previous image under Ephraim)

1870 Precinct 2, Greenup, Kentucky. Lists Josiah Morgan (age 30), and wife Melissa C. (age 31). Josiah is a farmer, Melissa is keeping house. (on the same census page is his brother Ephraim's family).

1880 Jefferson, Scioto, Ohio. Lists a J.S. Morgan (age 41), wife Melissa C. (age 42), a niece Catherine B. (age 16), a nephew Josiah (age 4). J.S. lists his father birthplace as PA and mother Ohio. He is a farmer.

1900 Valley, Scioto, Ohio. Lists Josiah S. (age 61 or 62-b.Sept 1838), Melissa C. (age 62-b. Jan 1838) Josiah S. had the occupation of undertaker, and marks his fathers birthplace as Pennsylvania and mother Ohio (both of which are inaccurate).

The nephew mentioned previously Josiah is listed after in another household. Josiah Jr. (age 27 -b.Dec 1872), Anna (wife age 22 -b.Sept 1877), Olive (daughter age 1 -b. Nov 1898), Ralph S. (son age under 1- b. Jan 1900). Josiah has an occupation of undertaker and liveryman.

1910 Clay, Scioto, Ohio. Lists Josiah (age 71) listed as a mayor of the village, wife Melissa C. (age 72)

1920 Clay, Scioto, Ohio. Lists Josiah (age 81) –he is widowed, listed as a watchman at the steel plant and living with his sons family (Joseph Morgan) which includes Joseph (age 45) who is a carpenter at the steel plant, Joseph's wife Anna (age 40), Arthur Armbrust (son in law to Joseph – age 22), Ruth Armbrust (daughter of Joseph – age 17), Josephine Morgan (daughter of Joseph – age 10), and Howard Morgan (son of Joseph – age 5).

On March 25, 1920 Josiah S. Morgan is reported deceased in Scioto, Ohio. (Ohio Death Records from 1908-1932, 1938-1944, and 1958-2007 page 335).

Death certificate of Josiah S. Morgan on March 25, 1920. Some crucial information is listed in this that was made by the informant Annie Morgan. Josiah was born on Sept. 27, 1838 in Columbiana Co, Ohio to John Morgan and Mary Long. This confirms the family was still in the area at that time. John Morgan was born in Wales his mother PA. This confirms what we have also gathered about John's birthplace.

g. Seventh Child of John and Mary: Sarah Catherine Morgan

Born: Apr 5, 1841 in Columbiana Co., Ohio

Died: September 16, 1895. Buried in Otway Cemetery, Otway, Ohio.

Married: Dec 31, 1861

Spouse: Henry J. Snyder

Married: Oct 9, 1867

Spouse: Andrew Jackson Salsbury/Saulsberry

Sarah Catherine and Henry Snyder had the following children:

1. Elizabeth "Betsy", b. abt. 1862; d. 1871. Cause of death asthma.

Sarah Catherine and Andrew Salsberry had the following children:

2. Jesse, abt. 1858.(possible child of Henry Synder)
3. Franklin, abt. 1860. (possible child of Henry Synder) 4. Margaret, b. 1862. (possible child of Henry Synder)
5. Robert W., b. 1869.
6. Ruth Ann, b. 1870.
7. James, b. 1872.
8. Jennie, b. 1874.
9. Otto, b. 1876.
10. Charles, b. 1878.
11. Hannah, b. 1881.
12. Olive Blanch, b. 1882.
13. Homer
14. Rachel
15. Roy

Timeline:

Dec 31, 1861 Marriage of Sarah Catherine and Henry Snyder.

1867-1869 Apparently Henry Snyder is either deceased or divorced Sarah Catherine.

Oct 9, 1867 Marriage of Sarah Catherine Morgan and Andrew Jackson Salsbury.

1870 Brush Creek, Scioto, Ohio. Andrew J. Salsbery (age 29), Sarah C. (age 29), Betsey

Snyder (age 7), Robert W. Snyder (age 1), Ruth Snyder (age under 1), Jessy Salbery (age 12), Franklin Salsbery (age 10), Margaret Salsbery (age 8). Andrew is a farmer, Jessy is farm laborer. (Andrew Jackson Salsbery parents are from Brush Creek).

1880 Union, Scioto, Ohio. Andrew Salsbery (age 41), Sarah (39), Jesse (age 20), Magges (age 17), Ann (age 10), James (age 7), Jennie (age 6), Otto (age 4), and Charles (age 2).

Sept. 16, 1895. Sarah Catherine is deceased.

h. Eighth Child of John and Mary: James Knos Morgan

Born: Jul 7, 1845 in Jefferson Twp.,Scioto Co., Ohio

Died: Mar 17, 1923 in Portsmouth, Scioto Co., Ohio. Buried in Lucasville, Ohio.

Married: Jun 12, 1871

Spouse: Margaret Desmond

Married: Aug 12, 1873 in Greenup Co., Ky.

Spouse: Anna Eliza England

(photo on left - James Knos and Anna with daughter and grandchild)

James Knos and Anna England had the following Children:

1. William James W., b. Apr 17, 1875 in Greenup Co., KY, d. Jan 28, 1962 in Portsmouth, Scioto Co., OH. Buried in Lucasville Cemetery.
2. Robert D./S., b. Oct 19, 1878 in Greenup Co., KY, d. Jun 9, 1945, m. Flora ?.
3. Mary C., b. 1879.
4. Bessie M., b. Dec 14, 1886 in Valley Twp., Scioto Co., OH, d. Mar 14, 1896, Died in infancy. Buried in Lucasville Cemetery.
5. Ida May, b. Feb 1889 in Valley Twp., Scioto Co., OH; d. Mar 3, 1978.
6. Julia E., b. Nov 1894 in Valley Twp., Scioto Co., OH, d. Nov 5, 1987.
7. Louisa "Lou", b. Sep 1883 in Valley Twp., Scioto Co., OH. Buried in Lucasville Cemetery.
8. Mary Katherine "Kate", b. Oct 18, 1879, Greenup Co., KY, d. Jul 31, 1941, White Cross Hosp., Columbus, Franklin Co., OH, death cause was

carcinoma of stomach. Buried at Memorial Burial Park. m. William H. Walcutt.

9. Pvt. John E, b. Jun 29, 1891, Valley Twp., Scioto Co., OH. Buried in Lucasville Cemetery, d. Oct 26, 1955. Served as an Ohio Pvt. - 572 Cassual Co., WWI.

Julia E. Morgan with unidentified man circa 1920's/30's leaning against a vehicles bucket seat (could this be her brother John who worked at a car shop?).

Timeline:

1870 Precinct No. 2, Greenup, Kentucky. James Knos (age 24) is a farm laborer living under the household of John Morgan Jr. (age 32).

Aug 12, 1873 James Knos Morgan married Anna Eliza England in Greenup Co., Kentucky.

1880 Globe School House, Greenup, Kentucky. James (listed as Jas – age 23), Ann E. (age 23), Jas W. (age 5), Robert D. (age 2), and Mary C. (age 8 months). James is a farmer.

1900 Valley, Scioto, Ohio. James K. Morgan (age 54 –b. July 1845), wife Anna E. (age 43 -b.1857), a son Robert D. (age 21 –b.Oct 1878), daughter Kate (age 19 - b.Oct.1880), daughter Lou (age 16 -b.Sept.1883), daughter Ida M. (age 11 – b.Feb 1889), son John E. (age 8 -b. June 1891), and daughter Julia E. (age 5 – b.Nov 1894). James married Anna in 1875.

1910 Portsmouth, Ward 1, Scioto, Ohio. James Knos (age 65), wife Annie E. (age 52), daughter May (age 21), John (age 18), Julia (age 16). James is listed as a laborer for shops, May and Julia work as a clerk at a shoe store, and John as a moulder for a store.

Anna Morgan with grandson Paul Morgan

1920 Portsmouth, Ward 4, Scioto, Ohio. James K. (age 76), wife Ana Eliza (age 64), Ida May (age 28), John E. (age 26), Julia E. (age 24). James is a laborer, Ida works as a stenographer at a steel plant, John is a boilermaker at a car shop, and Julia is a officeholder at the steel plant.

March 17, 1923 James Knos Morgan is reported deceased in Scioto, Ohio (Ohio Death Records from 1908-1932, 1938-1944, and 1958-2007 page 489).

Death certificate of James Knos Morgan on March 17, 1923. Again notice incorrect birth information for parents.

i. Ninth Child of John and Mary: Rev. Robert Dennison Morgan, D.D.

Born: Aug 27, 1842 in Columbiana Co., Ohio

Died: Dec 21, 1926. Buried in Greenlawn Cemetery in Columbus, Franklin Co., Ohio

Married: May 23, 1871 in Scioto, Ohio
Spouse: Julia Gephart

The Morgan Memorial Methodist Church on East Broad St. in Columbus was named in his honor, possibly as a founder. He was active in all aspects of church affairs (it is unclear where this church currently resides today, having either been torn down or renamed) and was a city missionary for Columbus. In 1914, Robert's poetry was published in journals including the Western Christian Advocate and wrote his first book entitled 'Poems of Life' that the church helped publish through New Franklin Printing Company. His first 1,000 books were said to have easily sold out. He was known primarily for his duties as a reverend in the Methodist Evangelical Church and was required to move around a lot before finally settling in Columbus, Ohio. Robert was named after his mother's sister's husband Robert Dennison.

Robert and Julia are thought to have had one child, a girl who died at birth.

Timeline:

July 1, 1863 Robert (age 21) was listed in the US Civil War Draft 11th Congressional District of Jefferson, Scioto, Ohio. Robert is listed as a schoolteacher for occupation and noted as single.

May 23, 1871 Marriage of Robert D. and Julia Gephart in Scioto, Ohio.

1880 Grove City, Franklin, Ohio. R.D. Morgan (age 37), wife Julia (age 39). Robert listed as a preacher. Robert incorrectly has parents both born in Ohio.

1900 Malta, Morgan, Ohio. Robert D Morgan (age 58 –b.Aug 1842), wife Julia D (age 60–b.Sep 1840). They were married in 1871. Robert is a minister.

1910 Columbus Ward 11, Franklin, Ohio. Robert D Morgan (age 67). Julia D (age 69), and sister in law Ida Gephart (age 62). Robert is a minister, working in a church.

1914 'Poems of Life' book is authored by Robert Dennison Morgan and published by a church in Columbus. Many of the poems are powerful and spiritual, from growing up in Ohio to the loss of their daughter (New Franklin Printing Company, 1914 - 53 pages). This beautiful book can be found among collectors and has a scanned digital copy available at http://catalog.hathitrust.org/Record/100216831

May 13, 1914 poem 'The Voice of the Red Bud' by the Rev. Robert Dennison Morgan, D.D., published in the Western Christian Advocate under the section 'Life in the Spirit.'

1915 'The Healer and His Robe, the Working Girl, and Other Poems' by Robert Dennison Morgan (New Franklin Printing Company, 1915 - 22 pages). Only 2 known copies in the Columbus area.

Unknown date, 'My Neighbor and Myself, and other poems' by Robert Dennison Morgan (New Franklin Printing Company, 19--? 16 pages). Only known copy available in the New York Public Library.

1920 Columbus, Ward 14, Franklin, Ohio. Robert Morgan (age 77), wife Julia (age 79) and niece Isabel Fisher (age 57) is living with them. Robert is a preacher and missionary.

Dec 21, 1926 Robert Dennison Morgan is reported deceased in Franklin, Ohio (Ohio Death Records from 1908-1932, 1938-1944, and 1958-2007 page 493).

DIVISION OF VITAL STATISTICS
CERTIFICATE OF DEATH

392 File No. 74193

1 PLACE OF DEATH
County _Franklin_
Registration District No. _392_ File No. _74193_
Township ________
Primary Registration District No. _8187_ Registered No. _4479_
or Village ________ No. ____ _Residence_ St., ____ Ward
or City of _Columbus_
(If death occured in a hospital or institution, give its NAME instead of street and number)

Did Deceased Serve in U. S. Navy or Army ________

2 FULL NAME _Robert Dennison Morgan_

(a) Residence. No. _980 Neil Avenue_ St., ____ Ward.
(Usual place of abode)
(If nonresident give city or town and State)
Length of residence in city or town where death occurred ____ yrs. ____ mos. ____ ds. How long in U.S., if of foreign birth? ____ yrs. ____ mos. ____ ds.

PERSONAL AND STATISTICAL PARTICULARS

3 SEX _Male_
4 COLOR OR RACE _White_
5 Single, Married, Widowed or Divorced (write the word) _Married_

5a If married, widowed or divorced
HUSBAND of (or) WIFE of _Mrs. Julia H. Morgan_

6 DATE OF BIRTH (month, day, and year) _Aug. 27, 1842_

7 AGE Years _83_ Months _3_ Days _24_ If LESS than 1 day ____ hrs. or ____ min.

8 OCCUPATION OF DECEASED
(a) Trade, profession, or particular kind of work _Retired Minister_
(b) General nature of Industry, business, or establishment in which employed (or employer) _M. E. Church_
(c) Name of employer ________

9 BIRTHPLACE (city or town) _Columbiana County_
(State or country) _Ohio_

PARENTS

10 NAME OF FATHER _John Morgan_
11 BIRTHPLACE OF FATHER (city or town) ________
(State or country) _Ohio_
12 MAIDEN NAME OF MOTHER _Mary Decker_
13 BIRTHPLACE OF MOTHER (city or town) ________
(State or country) _Ohio_

14 Informant _Mrs. Julia H. Morgan_
(Address) _980 Neil Avenue_

15 Filed _12/23 1926_ _J. W. Keegan_ REGISTRAR

MEDICAL CERTIFICATE OF DEATH

16 DATE OF DEATH (month, day and year) _Dec. 21, 19 26_

17 I HEREBY CERTIFY, That I attended deceased from _August_, 19 26, to _Dec 20_, 19 26, that I last saw him alive on _Dec 21_, 19 26, and that death occurred, on the date stated above, at _3.30_ m.

The CAUSE OF DEATH* was as follows:

Senility
(duration) _5_ yrs. ____ mos. ____ ds.

CONTRIBUTORY (SECONDARY)
(duration) ____ yrs. ____ mos. ____ ds.

18 Where was disease contracted if not at place of death? ________
Did an operation precede death? _no_ Date of ________
Was there an autopsy? _no_
What test confirmed diagnosis? ________

(Signed) _Ole Ross_ M. D.
_12-22 1926_ (Address) _1075 Oak St_

*State the DISEASE CAUSING DEATH, or in deaths from VIOLENT CAUSES, state (1) MEANS AND NATURE OF INJURY, and (2) whether ACCIDENTAL, SUICIDAL or HOMICIDAL. (See reverse side for additional space.)

19 PLACE of Burial, Cremation, or Removal _Green Lawn Cemetery_
DATE OF BURIAL _Dec 23-26_

20 UNDERTAKER THE EDWARD E. FISHER COMPANY,
ADDRESS _Columbus, O_

20a EMBALMER _Wesley Bodey_
LICENSE NO. _3159 A._

Death certificate of Robert Dennison Morgan on December 21, 1926. This confirms the John Morgan family was still in Columbiana Co. in 1842 based on his birthdate of August 27, 1842. Inaccuracies again in father and mother's birthplace.

a2 Child of Nathan and Lois: Oscar Winfield Morgan Sr.

Born: Jan 20, 1861 in Gailsburg, Illinois

Died: Sep 29, 1934 in Stuart, Iowa., buried in South Oak Grove Cemetery, Stuart, Iowa. Cause of death being Bright's Disease.

Married: Jun 26, 1907 in Stuart, Adair Co., IA. Spouse: Lily Mabel Pote

Lily was the daughter of Daniel Pote and Emma

Perkins. Lily was born Sep 16, 1887 in Menlo, Iowa, and died Feb 8, 1949 in Los Angeles, California. Buried in Forest Lawn, Glendale, California.

Lily described her husband, Oscar Winfield Sr., as the "town catch" being a successful attorney some 20 years older. Unfortunately, Oscar died shortly after the birth of their ninth child leaving the family destitute.

Oscar was also a farmer, and listed as such on his Stuart, Iowa death record. Oscar was buried in Block 13, Lot 29, Space 1 South Oak Grove Cemetery, Stuart, Iowa.

(Lelah and her sister Lily Mabel Pote)

Oscar Sr. and Lily Mabel Wedding honeymoon trip circa 1907.

Oscar and Lily Mabel Pote had the following children:

1. Nathan Wesley, b. May 13, 1908, Stuart, Iowa, d. Nov 16, 1915, Stuart, Iowa. Buried in Oak Grove Cemetery.

2. Lois Emma, b. Nov 29, 1909, Stuart, Iowa, d. Aug 11, 1994, Glendora, CA. Buried in Forest Lawn, Glendale, CA. (Haven of Peace section, Lot #785 space "In Loving Memory")

Lois and Nathan

3. Alice Marie, b. Apr 13, 1913, Stuart, Iowa, d. Nov 1, 1958, Los Angeles, CA. m. Robert Iles on July 28, 1940.

    a. Sharon Kay

Alice Morgan

4. Oscar Winfield Jr., b. Jun 24, 1915, Stuart, Iowa, d. Jun 26, 2001, Berea, Ohio.

    m. Margaret Emily Yoder on Aug 21, 1938 in Iowa City, Iowa.

    a. Clarion Joe Morgan

    b. Karen Marie Richards

Oscar W. Morgan Jr.

5. Clyde Nathan, b. Mar 22, 1917, Stuart, Iowa, d. Aug 2, 1987, Azusa, CA. m. Charlotte Warrington on Dec 23, 1939 in Little Brown Church, Nashua, Iowa.

    a. Ronald Nathan

    b. Dennis Clyde

6. Harold Wesley, b. Mar 15, 1920, Stuart, Iowa, d. Apr 10, 1963, Oakland, CA. Buried on April 15, 1963 in Golden Gate National Cemetery, San Bruno, CA. (Plot Y 486 SGT HQ 6230 HC INF) m. Emma Elnora Howard (during WWII) in Australia, Emma was b. Jul 19, 1919, Montana, d. Oct 11, 2002, Vacaville, CA. Buried in Upper Lake, CA.

7. Betty Jean, b. May 3, 1923, Stuart, Iowa, d. Nov 11, 1968, Indianapolis, Indiana. m. Fred Bonfils on Feb 1, 1950.

    a. Lynn Helene

    b. Peggy Kay "Bunny"

    c. Patrick Michael

    d. Frederick Walker "Fritz"

8. Roberta Mabel, b. May 2, 1925, Stuart, Iowa, d. Aug 22, 1976, Long Beach, CA. m. Thomas W. Watkins on Nov.25, 1941.

    a. Thomas W. Jr.

    b. Carolyn Jean

c. Cecelia Roberta

(L-R) Betty, Harold, Roberta

9. Robert Elwyn, b. Nov 19, 1926, Stuart, Iowa, d. May 23, 2005, Port Orchard,
   WA.

Timeline:

1915 Stuart, Guthrie, Iowa. O.W. Morgan (age 54) listed as married, an attorney, total earnings for 1914 from occupation $1,000. Education 8 years college. Value of farm $4,000. Church affiliate Methodist. Fathers birthplace Ohio, mothers New York. Has lived in Iowa for 33 years (having moved from Illinois to Iowa in 1882).

Jan 1, 1925 Lincoln, Adair, Iowa. Oscar W. (age 64), wife Mabel L. (age 37), daughter Lois E. (age 15), Alice M. (age 11), Oscar Jr. (age 9), Clyde N. (age 7), Harold (age 4), Betty J. (age 1) (Iowa State Census Collection, 1836-1925).

(L-R) Alice, Lily, Betty Jean, Lois, Clyde, Oscar Sr., Harold, Oscar Jr. circa 1924

a4 Child of Nathan and Lois: Delia Evaline Morgan

Born: Feb 17, 1855 in Galesburg, Ill.,
Died: Dec 11, 1926 in Stuart, Iowa.
Married: Jan 12, 1879 in Rio, Ill.

Spouse: James Edward Woodman

James Edward was the son of Thomas Woodman and Mary Adams. James was born Jun 16, 1851 in Rio, Ill., and died Mar 14, 1901 in Chicago, Ill.

Delia and James Woodman had the following children:

1. Lois Caroline, b. Mar 7, 1880, Rio, Ill., d. Jun 27, 1974, Plant City, FL.
2. Forrest Edward, b. Jan 4, 1884, Villisca, Iowa, d. Apr 11, 1962, Dexter, IA.

b1 Child of Ephraim and Elizabeth: Katherine Belle Morgan

Born: May 7, 1861 in Springville, Greenup Co., KY,

Died: Dec 31, 1921 in Portsmouth, Scioto Co., OH. Buried Jan 3, 1922 in Bennett Cemetery, Madison Twp., Scioto Co., Ohio. Cause of being Chronic Myocarditis.

Married: 1880

Spouse: Isaac Newton Mclaughlin

Isaac Newton was the son of James Mclaughlin and Hulda Brown. Isaac was born June 15, 1852 in Ohio, and died Sep 7, 1929 in Portsmouth, Scioto Co., Ohio. Buried in Bennett Cemetery, Madison Twp., Scioto Co., Ohio. (source 1900 Census Ohio Death Records, 1870 Census (Ephraim Morgan household), 1910 Census for Portsmouth wd.4, Scioto Co., OH, Newt. I. McLaughlin household, 1920 Census Portsmouth wd.4. Scioto Co., OH, Catherine McLaughlin household, 1880 Census Jefferson Twp., Scioto Co., OH, J.S. Morgan household).

Katherine and Isaac Mclaughlin had the following children:

1. Albert Newton, b. May 6, 1892, Harrison Twp., Scioto Co.,Oh, d. May 2, 1961, Scioto Co., OH. Buried in Bennett Cemetery, Madison Twp., Scioto Co., OH.

2. Cecil Morgan, b. Mar 1894, Harrison Twp., Scioto Co.,Ohio, d. Apr 25, 1935, buried in Bennett Cem., Madison Twp., Scioto Co., Ohio. Died in City Hospital, Springfield, Clark Co., OH. Cause of death was perforated gastric ulcer.

3. Emma, b. May 1898, Harrison Twp., Scioto Co., OH.

4. Florence Elizabeth, b. Feb 23, 1888, Harrison Twp.,Scioto Co., OH, d. Mar 8, 1937, Portsmouth, Scioto Co., OH. Buried March 10, 1937 in Minford, OH.

   Cause of death was carcinoma of breast. m. Henry Curnutte around 1909, Henry was b. Mar 1884, KY.(1920 resident of Oakland Ave., Wayne, Scioto Co., OH, 1920 occupation car repair for Norfolk Railroad, Sources 1900 Fed. Census Boyd Co., East Fork Magis terial District No. 2, Enumeration District 10, sheet 6B, 6/6/1900, Family 96, 1920 Census)

5. Harry, b. Apr 1896, Harrison Twp., Scioto Co., OH.

6. James William, b. Oct 12, 1881, Harrison Twp., Scioto Co., OH, d. Mar 10, 1949, Morgan Twp., Scioto Co., OH. Buried in Bennett Cemetery, Madison Twp., Scioto Co., Ohio. Cause of death was a Coronary Myocardial Insufficiency.

7. Lovell K., b. 1901, Harrison Twp., Scioto Co., OH.

8. May, b. Jun 1886, Harrison Twp., Scioto Co., OH.

9. Mervin R., b. 1903, Harrison Twp., Scioto Co., OH, d. 1904, Harrison Twp., Scioto Co., OH. Buried in Bennett Cemetery, Madison Twp., Scioto Co., OH.

10. Samuel C., b. Jul 1883, Harrison Twp., Scioto Co., Ohio, d. Jan 1, 1961, Portsmouth, Scioto Co., OH. Buried in Bennett Cemetery, Madison Twp., Scioto Co.,OH.

11. Sarah A. "Sadie", b. Feb 1890, Harrison Twp., Scioto Co.,Oh; d. Unknown25.

B2. Child of Ephraim and Elizabeth: James Ephraim Morgan

Born: Mar 1868 in Springville, Greenup Co, KY.

Died: Nov 9, 1935 in General Hospital, Portsmouth, Scioto Co., OH. Buried November 11, 1935 in Old Mackoy Church Cemetery, Siloam, KY.

Married: 1903

Spouse: Dora J. Elba

Dora was born Dec 1873 in Jefferson Twp., Scioto Co.,OH.

James was a farmer, who came to Logan County, IL with brothers Abner and William. James and Dora had one child born on Oct 4, 1904, that died before 1910 in childhood.

B4. Child of Ephraim and Elizabeth: Mary Ellen Morgan

Born: May 20, 1859 in Springville, Greenup Co., KY

Died Nov 23, 1924 in Springville, Greenup Co., KY. Buried on Nov 25, 1924 in Siloam Cemetery.

Married: Jan 2, 1876 in Greenup Co., Kentucky

Spouse: William Harrison "Harry" Craycraft

William Craycroft was the son of John Craycraft and Mary Griffith. William was born Jul 20, 1854 in Greenup Co., KY, and died Aug 20, 1915 in Springville, Greenup Co., KY. Buried on Aug 22, 1915 in Mackoy-Old Christian Church Cemetery. Mary

Ellen's cause of death was Chronic Intestinal Nephritis; brocho pneumonia. (Sources Census 1880 Globe School House, Greenup Co., KY 1900 census Springville Pct. Greenup Co., KY 1910 census, 1920 census, KY death recds. 1911 to present Ohio death recds. tombstone info.)

Mary and William Craycraft had the following children:

1. Anna Elizabeth, b. Sep 22, 1879 in Springville Pct., Greenup Co., KY, d. Nov 19, 1902.
2. James Walter, b. Nov 25, 1882 in Springville Pct., Greenup Co., KY, d. after 1932.
3. William Paul, b. Dec 26, 1884 (or 1886) in Springville Pct., Greenup Co., KY, d. May 3, 1961, Buried in Old Mackoy Cemetery, Siloam, KY.
4. Charles Abner, b. Nov 20, 1888 (or 1889) in Springville Pct., Greenup Co., KY, d. Apr 17, 1939, Scioto Co., OH. Buried in Mackoy-Old Christian ChurchCemetery.
5. Thomas Everett, b. Jan 1895 in Springville Pct., Greenup Co., KY, d. 1956, Siloam, KY.
6. Mabel Mae, b. Aug 31, 1898 (or 1902) in Springville Pct., Greenup Co., KY, d. Mar 2, 1943.
7. Nioma, b. Sep 23, 1878, Greenup Co., KY, d. Nov 11, 1878.
8. Harrison E., b. Sep 25, 1893, d. Jul 29, 1894.

B6. Child of Ephraim and Elizabeth: William H. Morgan

Born: May 10, 1862 in Springville, Greenup Co., KY.

Died: Dec 23, 1901.

Spouse: Frances

Frances was born about 1880. William H. is listed as a servant for the Joseph Fisher family in the Logan County, IL 1900 census.

William and Frances had the following children:

1. Eva, b. 1903, Mo.
2. Earl, b. 1909.

B7. Child of Ephraim and Elizabeth: Absalom M. "Abner" Morgan

Born: Apr 25, 1866 in Springville, Greenup Co., KY

Died: Jan 7, 1946 in Green Co. Infirmary, Greenup Co, KY. Burial Jan 10, 1946, Soloam Cemetery, Greenup Co., KY. Married: Oct 25, 1889 in Lincoln, Logan, IL.

Spouse: Mary Gertrude Swille

Mary Swille was born May 18, 1870 in Emden, Logan, IL, and died Aug 31, 1931 in Hartsburg, Logan, IL. Absalom was listed as Absalom M. in Logan County, and as Absalom F. in Greenup County. He was also known in both places as Abner.

Abner was born and raised in Greenup, Co., KY, and came to Logan County, IL before 1889. After he married, he moved back to Greenup County, KY. He and Mary Gertrude were never divorced. According to older family members, when his health went bad, he came back to IL, where he wanted to re-establish relationships with his children in Logan County. A couple of his daughters welcomed him, while the others rejected him because he abandoned his family. One of his daughters took him back to Greenup County, where he stayed until his death. Family rumor has it that he made his living as a gambler and horse trader (and trainer), and was also listed as a farmer while living in Logan County, IL. Abner died in the Greenup County Infirmary, where he had been a patient for 3 weeks. This is a home for the poor and infirm.

In 1920 census shows Gertrude living in Tazewell, Illinois

It appears that Abner left about 1915-16 based on the fact that Gertrude's Obituary stated she lived in Delavan, Ill for 16 yrs. and she died there. Mary Swille was buried in Union Cemetery, Hartsburg, Logan, IL.

Absalom and Mary Swille had the following children:
1. Myrtle, b. Jan 20, 1890, Hartsburg, Logan, IL, d. Jun 11, 1965.
2. Bert James, b. Jan 20, 1890, Hartsburg, Logan, IL, d. May 23, 1960, Hartsburg, Logan, IL.
3. Ethel, b. Feb 22, 1891, Hartsburg, Logan, IL, d. 1980, Lincoln, Logan, IL.
4. William Lyman, b. May 13, 1892, d. May 24, 1970. Burial in Union Cemetery, Hartsburg, Logan, IL. Never married.
5. Harry "Jack", b. Mar 27, 1894, d. Jul 22, 1969. Jack never married. He was crippled due to polio, and was left with a severe limp. He was known as a "happy-go-lucky" kind of person. Buried in Union Cemetery, Hartsburg, Logan, IL.
6. Russell, b. Mar 14, 1896, Logan County, IL, d. Dec 26, 1969, Tucson, AZ.

7. Mary Irene, b. Jan 19, 1898, d. Jan 03, 1983 in Methodist Hospital, Peoria, IL. Buried on Jan 6, 1983, in Peoria, IL. m. Harold Tracy, Apr 16, 1927. Harold was b. Jun 10, 1893, d. May 19, 1979, Green Valley, Tazewell, IL. Buried on May 22, 1979, Peoria, IL. Mary and Harold never had children. They ran a package liquor store in Peoria, IL.

8. Lillian Mae, b. Mar 11, 1899, d. Jul 1976, Plainfield, Will, IL.

9. John, b. Mar 1900.

10. Abner, b. Jul 24, 1901, Hartsburg, Logan, IL, d. Jul 8, 1962, Peoria, IL.

11. Clarence "Pat", b. Aug 5, 1903, d. Feb 1985.

12. Mildred O. "Babe", b. Jun 18, 1906, d. Sep 3, 1980, Pekin, Tazewell, IL. Buried in Prairie Rest cemetery, Delavan, IL. m. Charles F. Pomrenke on Sep 23, 1931. Charles was b. Dec 12, 1905, d. Oct 27, 1994, Pekin, Tazewell, IL. Buried in Prairie Rest Cemetery, Delavan, IL. Babe and Charlie never had children. They ran a tavern/restaurant west of San Jose, IL.

B8. Child of Ephraim and Elizabeth: Josiah Joseph Morgan Jr.

Born: Dec 25, 1872 in Springville, Greenup Co., KY.

Died: Aug 29, 1960 in Columbus, Franklin Co., OH. Buried on Sept 1, 1960 in Lucasville Cemetery.

Married: Sep 10, 1895 in Lucasville, Scioto Co., Ohio.

Spouse: Annie Shelpman

Annie was born Sep 2, 1879 in Wakefield, Pike Co., OH, and died Dec 30, 1973 in Columbus, Franklin Co., OH. Buried on January 2, 1974 in Lucasville Cemetery.

Josiah Joseph is the biological child of Ephraim and Elizabeth (Farmer) Morgan. When Elizabeth died, Joseph was adopted by Josiah and Melissa Catherine (Farmer) Morgan. Melissa was a sister to Elizabeth. It is not understood why such an event took place, but all tracking of Joseph is done through his biological parents.

Josiah Joseph and Annie Shelpman had the following children:

1. (infant), b. Aug 14, 1897 in Jefferson Twp., Scioto Co., Ohio, d. 1900, Jefferson Twp., Scioto Co., OH.
2. Olive Eliza, b. Nov 29, 1898, Valley Twp., Scioto Co., Ohio, d. Apr 30, 1998, Amherst, Lorain Co., OH.

Olive Eliza Morgan circa 1901

3. Ralph S., b. Jan 14, 1900, Valley Twp., Scioto Co., Ohio, d. before 1910.

4. Hazel Ruth, b. Apr 8, 1902, Valley Twp., Scioto Co., Ohio, d. Sep 21, 2002, Columbus, Franklin Co., OH.

5. Harry, b. Apr 19, 1904, Valley Twp., Scioto Co., OH, d. before 1910, Valley Twp., Scioto Co., OH.

6. Josephine, b. Nov 1909, Clay Twp., Scioto Co., OH. m. (1) (unknown) Kautz; m. (2) (unknown) KAUTZ (may be the same person).

7. Howard C., b. May 17, 1914, Clay Twp., Scioto Co., OH, d. Nov 1, 1974, Columbus, Franklin Co., OH, Buried in Lucasville Cemetery.

8. Charles E., b. Jan 9, 1916, New Boston, Scioto Co., OH, d. Apr 9, 1917, New Boston, Scioto Co., OH. Buried on April 11, 1917 in Lucasville Cemetery. Cause of death was Bronchopneumonia.

b11. Child of Ephraim and Elizabeth: Oliver D. Morgan

Born: Aug 17, 1882 in Springville, Greenup Co., KY, and

Died: May 10, 1944 in Butler Co., OH. Buried in Greenlawn Cemetery, KY.

Married: 1904

Spouse: Jessie L. Crull

Jessie was the daughter of David Crull. She was born 1881 in Scioto Co., OH, and died Sep 26, 1962 in Mercy Hospital, Portsmouth, Scioto Co., Ohio.

(source-1900 Census Springville, Greenup Co., KY Ephriam Morgan household, 1910 Census Portsmouth wd,3, Scioto Co., OH Oliver Morgan household, 1920 Census Portsmouth wd 1, Scioto Co., OH O.D. Morgan household 1930 Census Portsmouth wd 4, Scioto Co., OH Oliver d. Morgan household, Death records Note; Morgan, Oliver D. Date 5/10/1944, Butler Co., Cert. KY, tombstone)

Oliver and Jessie Crull had the following children:

1. EVA C., b. 1905, Portsmouth, Scioto Co., Ohio. Buried in Bennett Cemetery, Madison Twp., Scioto Co., Ohio.
2. Ollie O., b. 1908, Portsmouth, Scioto Co., Ohio. Buried in Bennett Cemetery, Madison Twp., Scioto Co., Ohio.

D2. Child of Ruth Ann and Abner Field: Sarah Ann Field

Born: Apr 27, 1854 in Scioto Co., OH.

Died Feb 19, 1930. Buried in Lucasville Cemetery, Lucasville, Scioto Co., Ohio.

Married: Mar 28, 1876 in Scioto, OH.

Spouse: Joseph Calvin McKinley

Joseph is a junior of Joseph McKinley Sr. Joseph was born Dec 14, 1855 in OH, and died Jan 3, 1930 in Scioto, OH. Buried in Lucasville Cemetery, Lucasville, Scioto Co., OH.

(Source-Census of 1860 of Scioto Co., OH Family Records supplied by Edith Fields, Jacobs/Plumb/Field researcher Family records supplied by Harold E. Clark, Family records supplied by Edith Fields for death)

Calvin McKinley and Sarah "Sadie" Field 50th Wedding Anniversary. (L-R) Mamie Flowers, Ellen Cook McKinley, Calvin McKinley, Sadie Field McKinley, Jerry Field.

Sarah Field and Joseph McKinley had the following children:

1. John Fisher, b. 11 May 1877; d. 15 Mar 1878.
2. Anna May, b. Jul 8, 1879; d. 1955.
3. Louis/Lewis Abner, b. Aug 18, 1881, d. Mar 20, 1956.
4. Joseph Walter, b. Mar 9, 1885.
5. Jesse Calvin, b. Nov 11, 1886, d. Apr 11, 1970.
6. Jacob Daniel, b. Feb 7, 1890, d. 1954.
7. Sarah Hazal, b. Oct 22, 1893, d. Sep 28, 1953, m. Arthur Branch Gilman, b. Nov 30, 1889, d. Sep 24, 1962.

Obituary for Sarah Field. (Mrs. Sarah Ann McKinley) Death twice within the past few weeks entered the McKinley home in Lucasville, Wednesday and claimed Mrs. Sarah Ann Field McKinley, widow of J.C. McKinley (Joseph Calvin died on January 3, 1930), prominent Valley Township resident, who passed away January 3 of this year. Mrs. McKinley died at her home in the village at 2:15 o'clock of complications following a stroke of apoplexy suffered several days ago. Mrs. McKinley would have been 76 years of age had she lived until April 27. She was born on Blue Run, Jefferson Township, and spent all her life in that community. She was one of the most highly respected residents of that section and her legion of friends will learn of her passing with genuine regret.
Surviving are five children, Mrs. Clyde Cook, Lucasville; Mrs. A Branch Dilman, of Mann, W. VA; Louis McKinley, cashier in the Lucasville Bank; Jesse McKinley, Lucasville mail carrier, and Jacob McKinley, school superintendent at McArthur. Mr. and Mrs. McKinley celebrated their 50th wedding anniversary several years ago. Mrs. McKinley was a member of the Lucasville M. E. church for years.

D3. Child of Ruth Ann and Abner Field: Jeremiah M. Field

Jeremiah "Uncle Jerry" Field and wife Joanna at opposite sides of photo, at back son Onno Field is sitting with wife Cora standing. Daughter of Onno and Cora sitting in baby stroller, her name is Mabel.

Born: Feb 28, 1856 in Scioto Co., OH.

Died: May 27, 1930. Buried in Lucasville Cemetery, Lucasville, Scioto Co., Ohio.

Married: Feb 15, 1883 in Scioto, OH.

Spouse: Joanna Arta Funk

Joanna is the daughter of Nicholas Funk and Lydia Gaul. She was born Sep 4, 1859 in Marion Twp., Pike Co., OH, and died Feb 6, 1937 in Lucasville, Scioto Co., OH.

Jeremiah was known to be well liked and respected within the Lucasville community.

Jeremiah Field and Joanna Funk had the following children:
1. Onno Field, b. Apr 16, 1884, d. Mar 1, 1976.

Obituary of Jeremiah Field – Twilight and the evening star of May 27, 1930, brought rest eternal to one of Lucasville's oldest and best beloved citizens, Jeremiah Field. Following his daily routine of duties, his daily meetings and jokes with his associates, and an errand of mercy a few miles out of town, this sudden summons was indeed a shock to his family and to the entire neighborhood. Although his health had been failing for some time, his cheerfulness and activity kept most of those with whom he mingled from realizing his serious condition. He was born February 23, 1856, on Blue Run, Scioto County, Ohio. A son of Abner and Ruth Morgan Field, who, with a sister, Mrs. Eliza Tomlinson, and a brother, John, preceded him in death many years ago.

February 23, last, he saw another sister, Mrs. J.C. McKinley of Lucasville, laid to rest. From that time, those who knew him best and loved him most were aware that he would soon join those gone before. Until about twenty-one years of age, he remained at home in the service of his family. A few years were spent in Illinois and Iowa. In 1883 he was married to Joanna Funk of Flatwoods Community. The young couple established their home in Illinois, where they remained five years and where one son, Onno, was born. Upon the death of his wife's father, they returned to the old homestead in Flatwoods, where they lived until 1924, when they came to Lucasville. Jovial and kindly, he quickly made friends. His honesty, integrity and sound principles made him a leader in his community, to whom everyone came for help and advice. Questions of importance were thoughtfully considered, but when once his decision was made, strong evidence was necessary to change his opinion. His great delight was to help others. His sisters learned early in life that he was indeed a friend as well as a brother; his heart and hands were ever extended to them. His last months were given largely to the task of leaving things in order for his faithful wife, son, and the grandchildren he loved so passionately, and who were the greatest joy of his declining years. His entire life is an example of outward practice of belief in Divinity and the brotherhood of man. The neighbor afflicted by sickness or death or any trouble was cheered and assisted by his help and sympathy. The church in need of help could always depend upon aid from him. Left to mourn their great loss are his wife, Joanna; his son, Onno, his daughter-in-law, Mrs. Cora Field, and the grandchildren, Mabel, Charlotte, Lois, Edith, Hazel, and Wilma Jean

Field; his sisters, Mary Ellen Field, Mrs. Melissa Shuman, Mrs. Rhoda Robinette, and Mrs. Nancy Clark. The memory of a generation of kindly helpfulness makes the passing of "Uncle Jerry" a deep sorrow to his many nephews and nieces.

D8. Child of Ruth Ann and Abner Field: Nancy Ann Field

James Clark and Nancy Field family: (L-R) Melvin C, Gladys C Young, Dexter C, Anna C Walker and Chessman C., sitting in front are James Clark and wife Nancy Field Clark

Born: Dec 4, 1867 in Jefferson Twp., Scioto Co., OH

Died: Mar 23, 1931 in Jefferson Twp., OH. Buried in Lucasville Cemetery, Lucasville, Scioto Co., Ohio.

Married: Oct 24, 1886 in Scioto, OH.

Spouse: James Melvin Clark

James Clark is the son of Charles Clark and Fatima Taylor. He was born Aug 1, 1867 in Porter Twp., Scioto Co., OH, and died Dec 15, 1919 in Jefferson Twp., Scioto Co., OH. Buried in Lucasville Cemetery.

(sources-Family records supplied by Harold E. Clark Marriage record, Scito Co., OH Vol. 7, p.158)

Nancy Field and James Clark had the following children:

1. James Melvin, b. May 6, 1898, Jefferson Twp., Scioto Co., OH, d. Oct 19, 1968, Portsmouth, Scioto Co., OH. m. (1) Anna May, m. (2) Ollie Rose/Ross, Jun 3, 1919, Scioto, OH, d. Feb 22, 1934, Scioto Co., OH.

2. Gladys Marie, b. Mar 28, 1902, Jefferson Twp., Scioto Co., OH, d. Mar 15,

   1974, Portsmouth, Scioto Co., OH. m. Harold Earl Young, Sep 16, 1922, Scioto, OH, b. Apr 13, 1901, Portsmouth, Scioto Co., OH, d. May 8, 1997, Portsmouth, Scioto Co., OH.

Sisters Gladys Clark Young and Anna Clark Walker, circa 1918

3. Dexter Henry, b. Aug 8, 1893, Jefferson Twp., Scioto Co., OH, d. Apr 14, 1963 (or 1962) Waverly, Pike Co., OH. Buried in Evergreen Cemetery.

4. Anna Lou, b. Nov 27, 1895, Jefferson Twp., Scioto Co., OH, d. May 19, 1920, Jefferson Twp., Scioto Co., OH. m. Ernest L.M. Walker, Oct 16, 1919, Scioto, OH, Ernest was b. 1896, Lawrence Co., KY, d. Dec 24, 1971, Portsmouth, Scioto Co., OH.

5. Carl Chessman, b. Sep 30, 1903, Scioto Co., OH.

6. Lois Morgan Clark, b. Jul 27, 1887, Jefferson Twp., Scioto Co., OH, d. May 24, 1973, Oxford, Butler Co., OH, m. Harry Ray Tharp, Dec 22, 1904, Scioto, OH, b. 1885, Ill., d. Jul 18, 1967, Butler Co., OH.

7. Sarah Jane "Jennie", b. Jul 15, 1889, Jefferson Twp., Scioto Co., OH, d. Nov 24, 1973, Oxford, Butler Co., OH, m. Stanley Imhoff, Butler Co., OH.

8. Fatima Ruth, b. Aug 3, 1891, Jefferson Twp., Scioto Co., OH, d. Oct 21, 1892, Jefferson Twp., Scioto Co., OH.

9. (infant), b. 1900, Scioto Co., OH, d. 1900, Scioto Co., OH.

James and Nancy Clark home on Blue Run circa 1912. Standing outside are Melvin, Gladys, Nancy, Chessman, Anna.

E1. Child of John Jr. and Elizabeth Gammon: Harriet Frances Morgan

Born: June 1, 1869 in Missouri

Died: Nov 16, 1940 in Kings Co., California

Married: abt 1888

Spouse: James Ellis, b. Aug 1860, d. before 1930 in Kings Co., CA

Harriet Frances Morgan and James Ellis had the following:
1. George Genevieve
2. Ruth
3. Raymond Harvey
4. Herbert Morgan
5. Helen
6. Annie Frances
7. Oscar Dean "Dean"
8. Robert Eugene "Gene"

E3. Child of John Jr. and Elizabeth Gammon: George W. Morgan

Born: Jan 1878

Died: 1930

Married: abt 1906

Spouse: Mabel E. Shay, b. abt 1890 in Nebraska, d. before 1930

George W. Morgan and Mabel E. Shay had the following:
1. Mildred G., born 1908 in Kings Co., California
2. Leroy John "Roy", b. June 15, 1909 in Kings Co., California, d. Jan 6, 1962 in San Luis Obispo, California

G6. Child of Sarah Catherine and Andrew Jackson Salsbury: Ruth Ann Salsbury

Born: 1870

Spouse: John Garvin

Ruth Ann Salsbury and John Garvin had the following:

1. Blanche Garvin.
2. Iva Lorraine Garvin.

H1. Child of James Knos and Anna England: William J. Morgan

Born: Apr 17, 1875 in Greenup Co., KY

Died: Jan 28, 1962 in Portsmouth, Scioto Co., OH. Buried in Lucasville Cemetery.

Married: Mar 6, 1899 in Greenup Co., KY. Spouse: Ida Warner

Ida was the daughter of Conrad Warner and Mary Daum. She was born Oct 9, 1879 (or 1880) in Scioto Co., OH, and died Sep 25, 1950 in Valley Twp., Scioto Co., OH. Buried in Lucasville Cemetery.

(Photo on left of James and Ida Morgan)

William Morgan and Ida Warner had the following children:

1. Mabel, b. May 17, 1900, Greenup Co., KY, d. Feb 23, 1972.
2. Isabelle, b. Feb 2, 1902, Greenup Co., KY, d. May 3, 1989. m. John Charles Violet, b. Nov 26, 1902, d. May 12, 1975.

(Photo on the right of Isabelle Morgan on her graduation day)

3. Paul H., b. Feb 7, 1904, Clay Twp., Scioto Co., OH, d. Jul 19, 1977.

Paul H. Morgan with his team of horses

4. Alma, b. Feb 18, 1908, Clay Twp., Scioto Co., OH, d. Apr 28, 1990, m. William Homer Long, b. Oct 8, 1906, d. Jan 6, 1979.

5. Geneva, b. Jan 24, 1910, Clay Twp., Scioto Co., OH, d. Sep 2, 1990. m. William Arthur Harness, b. Apr 5, 1908, d. Jun 6, 1967.

6. Anna May, b. Aug 18, 1911, Clay Twp., Scioto Co., OH, d. Jul 23, 2002, m. (unknown) Graves.

7. William Donald, b. Jun 29, 1915, Valley Twp., Scioto Co., OH, d. Dec 29, 2002. Buried in Lucasville Cemetery. m. Betty Carrel.

8. Andrew R., b. Jul 30, 1918, Valley Twp., Scioto Co., OH, d. Dec 14, 1996. Buried in Lucasville Cemetery.

"William and Ida Warner Morgan Family" includes: (L-R standing) Alma Morgan Long, Geneva Morgan Harness, Anna Morgan Graves, Andrew Morgan (who was blind), Paul Morgan, Mabel Morgan Bernthold Hickman, Isabell Morgan Violet, William Morgan. Seated William & Ida Warner Morgan.

Obituary for William J. Morgan read: William J. Morgan, 86, of Lucasville, died at 10:50pm Sunday at Portsmouth General Hospital. Mr. Morgan suffered a broken hip about 10 days ago and had been a patient at the hospital since that time. Born April 17, 1875, in Greenup County, Kentucky, he was a son of James and Anna England Morgan. Surviving are his wife, Amy Underwood, whom he married Sept. 10, 1951; five daughters, Mrs. Roy Graves, 1821 Highland Ave., Mrs. Charles Violet of Lucasville Rt. 2, Mrs. Mabel Bernthold and Mrs. Arthur Harness, both of Lucasville Rt. 4 and Mrs. Homer Long of New Holland; three sons, Paul of Lucasville Rt. 2, William of Lucasville Rt.4 and Andrew of Portsmouth; six stepdaughters, Mrs. Rosemary Flowers, 1818 Kendall Ave., Mrs. Cleo Keairns, 3341 North Taylor Ct., Mrs. Marie Mussetter, 1709 Eighth St., Mrs. Lillian VanDyke of Portsmouth Rt.6, Mrs. Margaret Douthitt of Piketon Rt.1 and

Mrs. Alma O'Brien of Tucson, Arizona; three sisters, Mae Morgan and Julia Morgan, both of 1526 Fourth St. and Mrs. Lou Williams of Columbus; 24 grandchildren and 26 great-grandchildren. Mr. Morgan was preceded in death by his parents, first wife, Ida Warner Morgan, who died in 1950, three daughters, two brothers and two sisters. Mr. Morgan was a retired farmer and a former representative of the federal land bank. He was a member of the Lucasville Church of Christ in Christian Union.

a2.3 Child of Oscar Winfield Sr. and Lily Mabel Pote: Alice Marie Morgan

Born: Apr 13, 1913 in Stuart, IA.

Died: Nov 1, 1958 in Los Angeles, CA. Buried in the Meditation section of Forest Lawn in Glendale, CA, lot 732 space 3a.

Married: July 28, 1940

Spouse: Robert Iles

Robert Iles was the son of Nicholas Iles and Katherine McCleary. He was born Jun 15, 1911 in Iowa, and died Apr 1, 1969 in Los Angeles, CA.

(Photo on left of Alice with daughter Sharon)

Alice and Robert Iles had the following child:

1. Sharon Kay Iles, b. Jul 20, 1941, Des Moines, IA. m. Edward F. Sharp in 1971, b. July 1, 1920, in Trinidad, CO, d. Sept. 24, 2007.

Alice with Robert Iles and daughter Sharon

a2.4 Child of Oscar Winfield Sr. and Lily Mabel Pote: Oscar Winfield Morgan Jr.

Born: Jun 24, 1915 in Stuart, Iowa

Died: Jun 26, 2001 in Berea, Ohio. Buried in Olmsted Memorial Park, North Olmsted, Ohio next to Margaret.

Married: Aug 21, 1938 in Iowa City, IA.

Spouse: Margaret Emily Yoder

(Photo above of Oscar and Margaret)

Margaret Emily Yoder was the daughter of Joseph Yoder and Marie Zillmer. Margaret was born Feb 20, 1918 in Wellman, Iowa, and died Mar 6, 1989 in Berea, OH. Buried March 8, 1989 in Olmsted Memorial Park, North Olmsted, Ohio.

Married: 1991 in Strongsville, Ohio. Spouse: Helen Schoenweeitz Velos. Helen was born Oct 3, 1915, and died Dec 27, 1997 in Berea, OH.

Oscar Winfield Jr. was a truck driver when he met Margaret who was working as a waitress in a small truck stop. He ordered coffee and she brought him coffee and cream. The cream turned out to be sour and he complained so she brought him another. Again the cream was sour and he made her replace it over again, but by this time the owner/operator had taken notice and fired her on the spot. Oscar felt bad and asked her out on a date since he was the cause of the problem. In a short three months they were married and that is the story they loved to tell.

Oscar was a mason, enjoyed sports, and loved to sing in the LaGrange Methodist choir. He also liked repairing things and was very mechanically inclined. During service with the Army, he rose to become a Sergeant, and commanded the actor Robert Mitchum. After this, he worked as a lineman and a corpsman operating large equipment to build the Alkan Highway in Alaska. Following this, he was a truck driver and worked for the county in Iowa as a maintainer of roads in and around Wellman, IA. While in Marion, he worked for the Caterpillar Company and then in Ohio for the Thew Shovel Company. After this he moved to Tennessee and then back to Ohio with Khoering Company (which bought out Thew Shovel). He decided to retire but that was short lived when he was asked to work for the Keystone School District as supervisor of custodial and maintenance. He did this partly to be near his grandchildren, whom he adored. Oscar always loved to travel and take trips in one of his many vans. Often with extended family, and this increased in retirement. He would travel cross-country stopping or driving by geological sites and visiting family. He was stern about avoiding tourist traps and had a deep appreciation to nature and sharing this love with others. Thankfully, he wrote a book of memoirs before his passing.

Margaret Emily Yoder was a descendant of Swiss Mennonite Amish. Her Yoder lineage goes back to the 16th Century in Canton Berne, Switzerland. She enjoyed gardening, sewing, crocheting, quilting, housekeeping, and conversation. She loved spending time with family, especially the kids, and had several pets over the years. She was active in the Methodist church in LaGrange, Ohio and their craft club, as well as a member of American Legion.

Oscar Winfield Jr. and Margaret Yoder had the following children:

1. Clarion Joe Morgan, b. Oct 28, 1939, Keokuk, IA. m. Carol Jackson on Jun 17, 1961 in Laporte, OH, b. Aug 18, 1941, Oberlin, OH.
2. Karen Marie Richards, b. 15 Dec 1946, Iowa City, IA. m. Jerry Lynn Richards on May 3, 1969 in LaPorte, OH, b. Sep 19, 1941 in Berea, OH.

Oscar Morgan and family visited the Morgan's in Southern California.

a2.5 Child of Oscar Winfield Sr. and Lily Mabel Pote: Clyde Nathan Morgan

Born: Mar 22, 1917 in Stuart, IA.

Died: Aug 2, 1987 in Azusa, L.A., CA. Buried in Forest Lawn, Covina Hills, CA.

Married: Dec 23, 1939 in Little Brown Church, Nashua, IA

Spouse: Charlotte Maxine "Mickey" Warrington

Charlotte "Mickey" was the daughter of Marshall Warrington and Gertrude Plummer. Charlotte was born Mar 27, 1919 in Des Moines, IA, and died Oct 24, 2009 in Azusa, CA.

(Source: 1920 Census for Des Moines Ward 7, Polk, Iowa Roll T625-509 page 13A Enumeration District 166 Image 856, Ancestry.com US Fed Census database on line Provo, UT)

Clyde and Charlotte Warrington had the following children:

1. Ronald Nathan, b. Jun 30, 1942, Des Moines, IA. m. Nancy Carole Purcell on Jun 27, 1964, b. June 2, 1939 in Matoaka, WV.
2. Dennis Clyde, b. Nov 26, 1947, Inglewood, CA, d. July 7, 2010 in Azusa, CA.

(Photo on right of Clyde and Charlotte)

a2.7 Child of Oscar Winfield Sr. and Lily Mabel Pote: Betty Jean Morgan

Born: May 3, 1923 in Stuart, IA
Died: Nov 11, 1968 in Indianapolis, Indiana.
Married: Feb 1, 1950
Spouse: Fred Bonfils

Betty and Fred Bonfils had the following children:

1. Lynn Helene Bonfils, b. Nov 3, 1950, Denver, Colorado.
2. Peggy Kay "Bunny" Bonfils, b. Nov 23, 1951, Indianapolis, Indiana.
3. Patrick Michael Bonfils, b. Mar 17, 1953, Indianapolis, Indiana, m. (1) Chris Perisho, m. (2) Mary Kay Turner, Jun 2, 1980, Indianapolis, Indiana, b. Feb 2, 1961, Indianapolis, Indiana.
4. Frederick Walker "Fritz" Bonfils, b. Dec 26, 1954, Indianapolis, Indiana.

a2.9 Child of Oscar Winfield Sr. and Lily Mabel Pote: Roberta Mabel Morgan

Born: May 2, 1925 in Stuart, IA
Died: Aug 22, 1976 in Long Beach, CA.
Married: Nov 25, 1941
Spouse: Thomas W. Watkins

Thomas Watkins was born Mar 20, 1923 in Arkansas, and died in Prescott Valley, Arizona.

Roberta and Thomas Watkins had the following children:
1. Thomas W. Jr. Watkins, b. Dec 6, 1945, Long Beach, CA.
2. Carolyn Jean Watkins, b. Feb 8, 1947.
3. Cecelia Roberta Watkins, b. Aug 24, 1951, Stuart, Iowa.

(Photo on right of Roberta and Thomas Watkins circa 1944/45)

a4.1 Child of Delia Evaline and James Woodman: Lois Caroline Woodman

Born: Mar 7, 1880 in Rio, IL

Died Jun 27, 1974 in Plant City, Florida.

Married: Dec 28, 1906

Spouse: Thomas Radford Agg

Thomas Radford Agg was born May 17, 1878.

Lois Woodman and Thomas Agg had the following children:

1. Muriel Lois, b. Nov 3, 1907, d. Apr 16, 2002, m. Samuel Cedric Whitehouse.
2. Alice Jane, b. Jun 10, 1911, d. Oct 13, 1968, m. John Flicklin, b. Aug 26, 1911, d. Oct 15, 1981.

a4.2 Child of Delia Evaline and James Woodman: Forrest Edwards Woodman

Born: Jan 4, 1884 in Villisca, Iowa

Died: Apr 11, 1962 in Dexter, Iowa.

Married: April 5, 1910 in Pittsburgh, PA

Spouse: Aida Florence Owens

Aida is the daughter of William Owens and Ida Jamison. She was born Oct 9, 1883 in Pittsburgh, PA, and died Feb 13, 1950 in Des Moines, Iowa.

Forrest Woodman and Aida Owens had the following children:

1. William Edward Woodman, b. May 11, 1911, Pittsburgh, PA, d. Mar 15, 1986, Winterset, Iowa. m. (1) Betta A. Burchfield on Sep 13, 1937 in Bethany, Missouri, b. Jan 22, 1919, d. Jun 11, 1998. m. (2) Phyllis Mae See, Jul 18, 1950, Austin, Texas, b. Nov 18, 1923.
2. Joseph Thomas Woodman, b. Jun 22, 1913, Pittsburgh, PA, d. May 17, 2001. m. Camilla E. White, b. Dec 7, 1914, d. Dec 8, 2000. (Joseph Thomas owned a Ben Franklin store in Stuart, IA. In 1960, a storm came through decimating the building.)
    3. Evelyn Jean Woodman, b. Jul 15, 1917, Stuart, Iowa, d. Jul 16, 1983.
    4. Lois Aida Woodman, b. Jan 8, 1919, Stuart, Iowa, d. Feb 1990.
    5. Florence Elizabeth Woodman, b. Jul 13, 1922, Stuart, Iowa, m. Francis Marion Krohn, Jun 30, 1946, b. Jun 22, 1916, Mound Prairie Twp., Iowa.
    6. Margaret Ethel Woodman, b. Mar 10, 1924, Stuart, IA. d. Jul 14, 1998. Buried in South Oak Grove Cemetery.

b1.10 Child of Katherine Belle and Isaac McLaughlin: Samuel C. McLaughlin

Born: Jul 1883 in Harrison Twp., Scioto Co., OH

Died: Jan 1, 1961 in Portsmouth, Scioto Co., OH. Buried in Bennett Cemetery, Madison Twp., Scioto Co.,OH.

Married: 1904

Spouse: Verna M. Clear

Verna was born 1887, and died Jan 7, 1964 in Southern Hills Hosp., Portsmouth, Scioto Co., Ohio. She was buried in Bennett Cemetery, Madison Twp., Scioto Co., Ohio.

Samuel McLaughlin and Verna Clear had the following children:

1. William Lloyd, b. 1904, Portsmouth, Scioto Co., OH, d. Oct 2, 1939, buried in Bennett Cemetery, Madison Twp., Scioto Co., OH.

2. Edward R., b. May 8, 1908, Portsmouth, Scioto Co., OH, d. Jul 2, 1981, Portsmouth, Scioto Co., OH. Buried in Bennett Cemetery, Madison Twp., Scioto Co., OH.

3. Pauline L, b. 1910, Portsmouth, Scioto Co., OH. Buried Bennett Cemetery, Madison Twp., Scioto Co., OH.

4. Esther L, b. 1913, Portsmouth, Scioto Co., OH. Buried in Bennett Cemetery, Madison Twp., Scioto Co., OH.

<u>**NOTES (of interest only):**</u>

History of Columbiana County, Ohio: with Illustrations and biographical sketches mentions the following Morgans and others of note:

- Page 34 Lewis Morgan
- Page 37 William D Morgan
- Page 50 Ann E.H. Morgan (attended a pioneer meeting in Hanover in 1877)
- Page 51 William D Morgan (attended an agriculture meeting in 1846)
- Page 57 William Morgan (part of militia group formed in 1806 – Capt William M'Laughlin Co. which was part of conflict that never arose, and disbanded in 1809)
- Page 77 Thomas Morgan (civil war)
- Page 81 Jason C. Morgan of Franklin Twp., mustered out on July 1865 (civil war). Page 84 Josiah B. Morgan, enlisted Aug 8, 1862; pro.capt. Jan 2, 1863. res. Jan, 13, 1864. (Skipping ahead of the civil war notes on page 89, 94).
- Page 114 Thomas J. Morgan (before 1840 practiced law in New Lisbon as an attorney, and went to Brazil as a US officer)
- Page 114 Clement Vallandigham became an attorney in New Lisbon
- Page 115 William D. Morgan, became an editor, publisher and printer in 1839 until
- 1852 (Centre/new Lisbon)
- Page 118 William D Morgan mentioned for school director elections (Centre/new Lisbon)
- Page 119 Jason Morgan – clerk of district for school (Centre)
- Page 127 J.B. Morgan (Centre) secret order society in 1865
- Page 141 Lewis Morgan – householders in 1828 (Fairfield)
- Page 142 Lewis Morgan – 1823 a trustee with Samuel Cowan, and Joseph Zimmerman
- Page 143 Joseph Morgan – 1863 businessman (Middleton, Fairfield, Columbiana)
- Page 148 Lewis Morgan – Hicksite Friends Meeting in 1832
- Page 154 Daniel Morgan was a Clerk in 1853 and 1854 (Franklin)
- Page 166 Anna Morgan mentioned as a lecturer in a secret society of 1872
- Page 186 John Morgan mentioned in a secret society in 1876
- Page 196 Thomas C Morgan (paid road tax in 1838 as a resident of Middelton)
- Page 239 William Morgan – 1869 Trustee (Salem)
- Page 268 Isaac Morgan – 1831 and 1832 trustee (Wayne)
- Page 268 John Morgan – 1846, 1847, 1848 trustee (Wayne)
- Page 269 Isaac Morgan voted in 1828 (Wayne)

- Page 269 John Morgan voted in 1828 (Wayne)
- Page 269 William Morgan voted in 1828 (Wayne)
- Page 270 Isaac Morgan noted as a Justice of the Peace (Wayne)
- Page 271 has a portrait of Jabez Coulson (West, Columbiana, Ohio)
- Page 284 Mr Morgan mentioned in connected to Wellsville Terra-cotta in 1874

Of Note - Franklin Twp was organized in 1816, upon 1832 with the erection of Carroll Co., Franklin was cut three rows of section on the west and also received an addition on the east of one row of sections, which were taken from Wayne Twp.

Of Note –Wayne was organized in 1806, and included originally a territory of six miles square, embracing thirty six sections. Upon the erection of Carroll County, in 1832, Wayne lost a row of sections to Washington on the south, and one to Franklin on the west, so that its area of territory is now included within twenty five sections, measuring five miles square.

AUGUSTA FRIENDS OR QUAKER MEETING HOUSE

History of Augusta Township_ by

Taylor C. Woodward

The Augusta Society of Friends was a branch of the Sandy Spring Society of Friends.

Sandy Spring Meeting House was located about one mile west of Hanoverton, in Columbiana County, and was one of the oldest meeting houses in the vicinity. It was built by a group of Friends, Stephen McBride, initiating the move to erect a log meeting house and school house in 1807. Later in 1827, to accommodate the growing congregation, a brick meeting house was built, which was used for more than half a century. Stephen McBride later came to what is now Augusta Township, Carroll County, having received a patent deed in 1820, from the U.S. Land Office at Steubenville - James Monroe, President, for the S.E. 1/4 of Sec. 2, Township 15, Range 5. (The writer of this having this deed in his possession.) A burying ground adjacent to the meeting house, above mentioned, is the final resting place of three soldiers of the American Revolution: Stephen McBride, Andrew Milbourn, and William Skelton, all familiar names in the early history of Augusta Township. Jonathan Dean, James McBride, Jabez Coulson and Jeremiah McBride, having been appointed at Sandy

Spring monthly meeting to take a deed in trust for a lot of ground, in what is now Carroll County, on which Augusta Meeting House was later built. And they accordingly took such deed from James McGowen, Dec. 12, 1818, for one acre of ground, located in the N.W. corner of the N.W. 1/4 of Sec. 2, Twp. 15, Range 5. (He having received a patent deed from the government in 1816 for the N.W. 1/4 of Sec. 2, Twp. 15, Range 5.) This for the use of members of Augusta Meeting and Sandy Spring Monthly Meeting when held at Augusta Meeting House. The same committee also received a deed in trust, from David Haldeman and Ann his wife, Oct. 12, 1825, for one acre of land, adjoining the one acre they had received in 1818, on the north side. On the latter, a school house had been built in 1810, and was called the Augusta "Friends" School House. This is the earliest school house in the vicinity, of which a record has been found. The schoolmaster was Nathan Pim, who passed away in 1816 and was laid to rest near the school house, and is said to be the first person buried in the "Friends" or Quaker Cemetery. Oct. 27, 1840, the above named committee transferred both lots to the new trustees appointed: Taber Coulson, Mahlon Hole, James Chambers, and David Haldeman. A meeting was held by the trustees and others June 13, 1840 at which time and place, it was decided to build a log meeting house, with donation labor, on the lot bought for that purpose. Work was commenced June 18, 1840, and continued as time permitted, until it was completed in the fall of 1841. Meetings were held in this building by the Friends or Quakers, for many years, where silent worship was held. To many, the pioneer Quaker's way of worship was unusual. Their meeting begins, not with a hymn or any formal opening whatsoever, but by those who have met to worship God, settling themselves in silence to self examination, meditation and secret prayer, the men usually on one side of the room and the women on the other. The stillness thus begun, may continue for a longer or a shorter period, possibly during the whole meeting, for it may please the Lord, or leaders that no word be spoken. Often however, some are given messages by Him to deliver. When any are thus led to speak, they rise and express their message, from whatever part of the building they may be in, or if anyone feels called upon to offer vocal prayer, he or she kneels, while the congregation rises and remains standing till the prayer is ended. When the meeting for worship has continued as long as those, sitting at the head of it think profitable, they turn to each other and shake hands, which act, while expressing the renewed bond of Christian fellowship, marks the conclusion of the meeting. No musical instruments were used in their meetings, in the old meeting house. One of the early customs of the Friends, was burying the Friends in rows instead of family lots, and some using sandstone for a marker, with only their initials and date cut on it. Having held meetings in the old Meeting House for thirty years and more, the congregation having continued to increase as time passed by, and many changes having taken place, in 1876, it was decided to build a new and larger brick meeting house, which was completed and ready for occupancy Feb. 20, 1877. This Meeting House is remembered by many of the present generation. The building being heated by a large round heating stove on each side of the room, and lighted by a large chandelier or ring of oil lamps, hung from the ceiling on each side of the room, also an oil reflector lamp on the wall, back of the minister, on each side. The back row seats being raised one step higher than the rest. Many of the regular members had stalls built with a roof over them, for the protection of their horses from the weather, while at the meetings. These meetings were well attended around the year 1900, for many years before and after, and the house was filled to overflowing many times. Meetings have been held outdoors in a tent, when the meeting house would not hold the crowds, which attended special meetings, which were held at times. One of the many changes made, was the use of the organ, in their meetings. Protracted meetings were held at times, with special speakers. Regular ministers were had for a period of time. After an extended period of time, as many of the old Friends had passed away, and some had moved away, and not enough members remaining to keep up the Meeting House, and as the roof was in need of repairs, they decided rather than take a chance of it being desecrated by vandals, they would have the building taken down, which they did about 1946. The cemetery marks the location, which is partly in Carroll, but mostly in Columbiana County, and is well taken care of by the Trustees of West Township, Columbiana County.

Immigration Record for a John Morgan - leaving the Liverpool port to Philadelphia on August 20, 1817

John Morgan b. 1777

Catherine b. 1778

Jeremiah b. 1803

John b. 1801 (is this our john? if so, then this would be his family) Jane b. 1805

Josiah b. 1808

Edmund b. 1810

Elizabeth b.1812

Ann b. 1814

Sarah b. 1817

According to the Giddens Shrum Family Tree on Ancestry.com (owner peacegodspeed) there is assumingly the same - John Morgan b.1777 from Montgomeryshire, Wales, d. Ohio. He married a Catherine Jones b. 1778.

-They had a son named Josiah Morgan b. July 20, 1807 in Montgomeryshire, Wales, Josiah married Martha Patsy Runnels Reynolds (1805-1894) in 1827 in Greene, Tennessee. Josiah residence in 1850 was Madison, Missouri. Then In 1880 residence was in Little Sioux, Harrison, Iowa. Death in Aug 1881 in Monona, Iowa.

-This would mean if this record relates to the immigration record and if our John is the brother of Josiah and son of John and Catherine, then John and family were from Montgomeryshire, Wales.

Is the elder William Morgan of Wayne, Columbiana a father to John or Uncle (see notes)? We do know that he had a John, Isaac, and William that was not related directly at least, and caused me some confusion in if this was our John or not but what about the possibility of an elder William having two or three sons named John? Maybe possible, but also maybe likely that our John is not related and moved directly from PA. Family Trees on ancestry.com list these trio Morgan brothers but do not include our John in them.

One of the Morgan families that is so often confused with our John Morgan because of his birthdate is John Morgan (b.1751 Chester, PA, d. Dec.13, 1835 in Edgemont, Chester, PA) and Rebecca Porter who had a son John Jr. born August 18, 1801 in Chester, Pennsylvania, along with . His parents were James (b. 1721 in Abington Twp., PA, d. July 2, 1799 in Chester, PA) and Ann Heacock (b. Dec. 11, 1718 in Philadelphia, PA, d. Dec.28, 1797 in Chester, PA).